SHADES OF GREEN

Adwoa Returns

By Judith Green

WTL INTERNATIONAL

SHADES OF GREEN

Published by
WTL International
930 North Park Drive
P.O. Box 33049
Brampton, Ontario
L6S 6A7 Canada
www.wtlipublishing.com

978-1-927865-31-6

Distributed in Ghana by:
Stephen Brobbey 024-460-5253 / 026-260-5253;
Enviroteck Enterprise 020-816-7075

Dedication

Shades of Green is dedicated to the youth of Ghana as an inspiration for them to safeguard Ghana's bountiful natural resources. Ghana's youth will inherit the mantle of environmental stewardship to protect, preserve and conserve Ghana's flora, fauna, water bodies, land and minerals while affording her the opportunity to prosper from them.

———

We would like to acknowledge funding support from the Ontario Arts Council, an agency of the Government of Ontario.

ONTARIO ARTS COUNCIL
CONSEIL DES ARTS DE L'ONTARIO

an Ontario government agency
un organisme du gouvernement de l'Ontario

Photo Credits

Front cover photo
(boy on the left and girl in the middle)
by Dr. Dennis Laumann

Front cover photo
(girl on the right)
by United States Agency for International
Development
(Public Domain)

Front cover photo
(forest background)
courtesy of John Bilous
@ 123RF.COM

Table of Contents

1

The Journey Back Home

The months had turned into weeks, then days, and finally the time came for Adwoa, her mother Faith, her father Sam and her brother Ebo to return to Ghana. Adwoa wasn't sure if she was ready for the trip back to Ghana. She would miss her friends and living in Toronto a lot. She was leaving a place that she loved and where she had spent the greater part of her life.

The family was scheduled to fly from Toronto via Washington, D.C. to Accra. Once the family arrived at the airport, they printed their boarding passes and then checked in their luggage at the airline counter. Afterwards, they went through security and then headed to their designated gate.

Once on the plane, Adwoa sat in the seat next to the window. One thing that she was excited about was to see the sights outside of the plane. Adwoa was too young to remember when she left Ghana and travelled on a flight with her family via Amsterdam to Toronto. She checked out how the seatbelt worked by fastening, tightening and loosening it. She noticed the small television screen overhead and the tiny monitor that was affixed to the back of the seat in front of her. She saw people adjusting their seats and with Ebo's help she was able to recline her seat.

Adwoa asked, "What are those things for?" pointing at some knobs above. Ebo demonstrated how the knobs worked. "This one is to control the air and the other one is to turn on and off the light. You push this button if you need assistance from a flight attendant," he explained. Adwoa plugged her headphones into the armrest of the seat she was sitting in and flipped through the radio stations and TV channels.

It took about thirty minutes for all of the passengers to put their carry-on luggage in the overhead compartments and under the seats and to settle down. The flight attendants readied themselves, the plane and passengers. Outside on the tarmac, workmen loaded luggage into the cargo hold while other workers put fuel in the plane. Meals that would be served later were brought into the galley of the plane on trolleys. The door of the plane was finally closed and all of the workmen and vehicles moved away from the plane so that it could prepare for takeoff. Everyone was asked to fasten their seatbelts and sit in an upright position.

The plane's engine revved up and finally, the plane started to move. It reversed slowly from the jet bridge and taxied towards the runway. Meanwhile, the passengers were briefed about safety on the aircraft. The captain spoke through an intercom and welcomed the passengers aboard the flight. He told them how long the flight would take, the altitude at which the plane would fly and the weather conditions for the flight path.

The plane taxied on the tarmac and waited in line behind other planes to takeoff. After about fifteen minutes, the plane got into position on the runway. The plane halted, its engines were cranked up and then it thrust forward with great force like a sprinter taking off on a one-hundred-metre dash. It sped down the runway faster and faster and then lifted into the air. The plane quickly began to ascend and soon pierced through the sky.

Through the window, Adwoa saw Toronto below basking in the soft, summer-evening sun. Splashes of green lawns and trees between high-rise buildings lined the orderly network of streets and intertwining highways. Adwoa tried to see if she could locate the position of her home for one last look—a final farewell—but the plane turned and headed south over Lake Ontario to the US border. It was a smooth and short flight which lasted just under an hour and a half.

At the airport in Washington, D.C., hordes of travellers moved hastily to catch connecting flights or to head home after returning from trips. Other travellers waited patiently at their scheduled gate areas. Adwoa and her family waited for two and a half hours in the passenger lounge. There was a fragile-looking elderly woman with a medium-sized frame sitting next to Adwoa. Rhythmically, she glanced at Adwoa—every few seconds, it seemed. Eventually, their eyes met and Adwoa smiled. Adwoa intently looked back and had a chance to study her face. Her eyes looked kind and her wrinkles, from years and years of smiling, were endearing.

"What's got you so down, young lady?" the woman pried in a soft and sweet voice.

"Nothing ma'am. I'm okay, thank you," Adwoa said.

"You know, everything that happens on this earth happens for a reason. Everything has its purpose," the lady said. Then she excused herself and was off.

That's nice! Adwoa thought, *but how strange? That lady doesn't know about my life. What did she mean?*

Adwoa was nervous when the agent at the counter next to the boarding gate announced that it was time to board the plane for their flight to Accra. It was pretty much official. She was Ghana-bound and couldn't look back. Adwoa and her family grabbed their carry-on luggage and got in line to board the plane. When they boarded the plane, they all sat in the same row. Adwoa sat in the window seat, Ebo sat next to her and Faith sat in the aisle seat beside him. Sam sat in the seat across the aisle from Faith.

SHADES OF GREEN

The plane left on time at 11:30 p.m. As the plane took off, Adwoa looked at Washington below, with its brightly lit sky scrapers, streets lined with lights and vehicles driving back and forth on distant roads. The bright lights and enchanting view afforded by the plane's window were not enough to cheer up Adwoa. Within a few minutes, Washington faded in the surrounding darkness outside. The plane continued to ascend steadily to its intended altitude and then forged ahead towards its destination across the wide Atlantic Ocean.

During the long flight, it began to sink in that it was a time of great change. Adwoa wasn't going on a vacation where she would return home to Toronto after a few weeks. It was goodbye to a way of life that she enjoyed and loved. Thoughts of her friends and their last get-together flooded Adwoa's mind. *What a crazy bunch! How I'll miss them!* she thought. There was Amma, the wisest because she was the oldest—by a mere two months; then there was Joy, the funny one; Shawn, the know-it-all; Sarah, the fashion queen; and Pam, the shy one. Tears began to trickle down Adwoa's cheeks. There was something else also tugging at Adwoa's heart. She had a love—a passion back home in Toronto.

As she turned to peer through the window of the plane to let her thoughts travel as far and wide as the plane in the air, she saw her own reflection. It mirrored her inner feelings of a sense of loss, sadness and an uneasy quiet. She skirted around the real issue in her mind. *I will have to find new friends in Ghana. Everything will be new. That's intimidating and scary*, she thought. Just before she pulled the window shade down, Adwoa saw the bright, full moon stationed in splendor in the sky amidst twinkling stars. She likened it to a bride surrounded by her cheerful bridesmaids on her blissful day.

Soon after, meals were served. The warm, tender chicken and seasoned potato balls just the way she liked them begged Adwoa to crack a smile, but she wouldn't budge. Adwoa knew she could get used to a new life but the love that was tugging at her heart as she thought of leaving life in Canada was her passion for preserving the planet. Adwoa had found a special place as part of the **green** group at her school back in Toronto.

Canada had a number of issues to be improved and she knew about them all. Ghana on the other hand, was natural and pristine—or so she thought. Just what would she do to help the planet there? Adwoa thought and thought until she drifted off to sleep while trying unsuccessfully to focus on a movie that was playing.

About four hours later, Adwoa woke up to the muffled sounds of chatter as passengers began to stir. The flight attendants were moving up and down the aisles, getting ready to serve breakfast to half-awake passengers.

"Did you have a good sleep, Sleepyhead?" her dad leaned over and asked.

"I had a little bit of sleep but I am still very tired. I wish that I could get some more," Adwoa replied.

"We will all have to catch up on sleep later," Sam said.

Ebo though, was still fast asleep.

When the captain announced that the plane was descending as it was approaching Kotoka International Airport in Accra, he asked the passengers and the flight attendants to prepare for landing. He said that the weather in Accra was bright and sunny at a temperature of 27°C.

When Adwoa pulled up the window shade, she saw a blue and sunny sky full of inviting clouds of differing shapes and density. Adwoa remarked, "The fluffy white clouds and blue sky look like the playground of angels and fairies."

It was just moments later when Adwoa saw that the plane was approaching a landmass. It was Africa, the Motherland, Ghana, home. She actually began to feel excitement just like her parents who were happy to be arriving back home. The plane descended gradually, bobbing a little while passing through a layer of thick clouds, a dense mist, and then through some thin cotton candy-like clouds. Closer to Accra, it was a clear and sunny day. As the plane approached the airport, Adwoa saw reddish-brown ground below. It suddenly looked familiar.

The plane continued its steady descent until it touched down on the runway, vibrating as it was reined in to reduce its speed. Thankful passengers cheered to celebrate the safe landing of the plane at its destination. The plane then taxied to its final stop and passengers prepared to disembark.

Adwoa stood at the doorway of the plane trying to mentally prepare herself to set her feet on Ghanaian soil again. As she glanced at the airport terminal and its surroundings, a wave of heat rushed to welcome her. The hot air embraced Adwoa and reminded her that she was in a tropical country.

It was mid-afternoon and the blazing sun gazed down from a clear blue sky. In the distance, tall and slender coconut and palm trees jutted out from the horizon. Their still, floppy leaves showed that they were abandoned by breezes.

"Finally, we're here, approximately *fifteen and a half hours* after leaving Toronto," Adwoa moaned as she and her family boarded the bus that was waiting to take them to the arrival lounge.

"Never mind time," Sam said jokingly. "Don't you know we have lost four hours of precious time because Ghana is four hours ahead of Toronto?"

Adwoa smirked.

The family's documents were processed by immigration officials and their baggage was cleared through Customs without much delay. The tired bunch emerged to the warm welcome of cheerful family and friends who came to the airport to greet them. Adwoa began to soften just a little inside.

2

A Taste
of Accra

Adwoa's family set out in a SUV for Adenta. Her family was going to stay at her uncle's place for three weeks until their own house was ready. Memories of Ghanaian life flashed back as Adwoa saw street-trading taking place everywhere. She vaguely remembered seeing street-trading before she left Ghana at the age of four. Along the crowded route, many businesses and colourfully painted roadside kiosks displayed all kinds of goods for sale. On the main roads, traders weaved between lanes of stopped and slow-moving traffic to sell their wares. A few of the traders seemed very young, as though they belonged in a classroom.

The scenes along the way were a stark difference from life back in Toronto. The change was dramatic. In Toronto, street-selling was illegal and not tolerated. The traders in Accra were selling goods like newspapers, toilet paper, phone cards, sachets of water, snacks, a variety of gadgets and all kinds of food and personal supplies. Traders acted like mobile stores by bringing goods to customers—the ultimate in shopping convenience.

"Ma, Accra is very busy. There are so many people and there is so much traffic. It is dangerous for traders to move between vehicles. Won't they get hit?" Adwoa asked.

"These traders are used to it, Dear," Faith replied.

"It is their livelihood so they won't stop even though it is dangerous," Sam added.

Adwoa observed, "It looks like such hard work. The traders carry goods around all day, mostly on their heads and in the hot sun. Some of them carry goods in their hands and in their arms too. It is not safe for them to breathe harmful exhaust emissions from vehicles either." This was the usual Adwoa. She was very thoughtful and always observant about the environment around her.

Traffic flowed slowly to avoid potholes and bumpy roads and crawled from congestion at times. Many tro tros (minibuses), bedecked with religious signage, were packed with people and helped to cripple traffic.

Adwoa admired the full array of brightly coloured, beautiful and interestingly designed clothing that people wore. The buildings were noticeably low which made the Accra skyline more visible than Toronto's with its jungle of skyscrapers.

When they arrived at her uncle's house, Adwoa wasted no time in updating her friends back in Canada about her journey. She let them know that she had arrived safe and sound. Adwoa was already beginning to feel the physical distance between them.

After having a shower and several hours of sound sleep, Adwoa woke up feeling refreshed. She quickly became aware of the elevated noise level of her new surroundings, especially the constant tooting of car horns. Anxious drivers tooted their horns frequently to signal to other drivers as they navigated the roadway. She soon realized that car horns were not only used to alert other drivers and pedestrians about drivers' intentions, but to greet people as well.

Adwoa and her family eventually moved into their own home in Dzorwulu Residential Area. Dzorwulu is located in the Greater Accra Region in which Accra, the country's capital, is located. On the third night at their own home, the electricity suddenly went off like it did twice before at her uncle's place. Adwoa now figured that it was not a rare occurrence. A generator was not yet installed at their home to use as a backup for electricity. No one could remember where to find candles or solar lights, so the family sat through the dark with glimmers of light from their cell phones.

Sam said, "So we must learn to appreciate electricity. In Canada, we were never worried about losing access to electricity. Our concern was rather about not wasting it. Who can forget having Adwoa as our very own in-house 'light police' who wouldn't let us leave the lights on unless we needed them? At times, we will wish that we had that dependable supply of electricity. But like everything else, people seem to get used to it and we will too."

Ebo remarked, "Ghanaians even have a name for the erratic electricity supply. They call it 'dumsor dumsor'."

Faith chuckled, "Ghanaians have a name for everything. They try to make light of the situation. "Dum" means off and "sor" means on.

Adwoa asked, "What causes the electricity to go off so frequently?"

Sam explained, "It's caused by low water levels at the Akosombo Dam where most of the electricity comes from; from too much demand for electricity and from faulty equipment and its maintenance.

"They are building thermal plants and developing solar energy to help generate electricity, plus they found oil offshore so once more gas production comes on stream, it should help the situation with the supply of electricity. Ghana, like Canada, is blessed with many resources including rivers and lakes from which **hydroelectricity** is produced. However, Ghana's water bodies are dwindling and becoming increasingly polluted."

Adwoa's ears started to perk up. She commented, "It is a problem when you want to use computers and charge cell phones. Even foodstuff will spoil easily when there isn't electricity for the fridge to work."

"It couldn't come soon enough for me," Faith remarked. "In a way, Ghanaians are lucky in that they still preserve a lot of their foods by salting, smoking, drying and fermenting, so it is less perishable. People have found ways to cope with the disruption in electricity. The use of gas stoves rather than electric ones to cook food helps the situation.

Ebo remarked, "It's strange that solar energy isn't used to generate electricity more when Ghana is blessed with so much natural and free sunlight.

"Let's pray for a solution to the electricity problem soon," Sam said. "Otherwise, how is everyone settling down? I hope that you aren't missing Toronto too much."

Ebo answered, "I am bored to death."

"If I were in Toronto at this time, I would be suffering from hay fever. I don't miss that part at all," said Adwoa. A little bit of an upbeat attitude was setting in. Just as Faith thought she was letting her guard down, Adwoa added, "But I miss my friends and shopping a lot. I also miss the long hours of daylight during summer that we enjoyed in Canada."

Faith suggested to Ebo, "Why don't you invite some of your cousins over or visit them since you don't know anybody else."

"You have already downloaded the chat App so that you can keep in touch with your friends in Toronto for free," Sam reminded Ebo.

Sam calculated, "As for you Adwoa, you will have less shopping to do because you will be wearing uniforms to school and you won't need a separate set of clothes for the fall and winter weather. Plus, you brought plenty of clothes to last you for a while,"

Later when the lights came back on, Sam remarked, "You see, not having light wasn't so bad after all. It gave us the opportunity to catch up on things. I am sure everything will be fine when we finish settling down. Anyway kids, you will be very busy soon, once school starts."

Plastic Garbage Everywhere

The following Saturday, Adwoa accompanied her mother to the Makola Market, a crowded outdoor market, to buy foodstuffs. The market was teeming with indoor stalls and outside many vendors were selling their wares under the shade of large picnic umbrellas. The market was bustling with activity. It seemed as though most people everywhere were involved with selling something.

Faith and Adwoa first came to the part of the market where business was brisk with goods such as secondhand clothing, electronic equipment, spare parts, tools, handbags, shoes, jewellery, fabric, household décor and gadgets.

Adwoa remarked, "The used goods business caters to customers who can't afford new stuff but it's a great way of recycling and reducing waste."

As they headed to the indoor market to shop for fruits and vegetables, Faith explained, "Yes, used goods help in that way but we should be careful with the amount of imported used goods. It burdens us with having to get rid of extra waste since the goods have to be thrown out after we use them. We already have challenges with our own waste."

Adwoa said as she weaved her way through the throngs of shoppers, hawkers and their booths, "This is like a department store and grocery store all in one. They seem to sell everything that you can think of in this market." Adwoa was beginning to discover a new appreciation of the problems that once seemed so straightforward from a distance.

At the indoor market, they were able to walk more freely without fear of getting separated. As they strolled through the market, the hawkers competed for their attention with the hopes of getting Faith to buy from them. When Faith and Adwoa approached a table of firm, red and juicy tomatoes stacked high, Faith was interested in buying some but she was reluctant to bargain for a lower price. Instead, the hawker added a few more tomatoes and reduced the price of the peppers she was also buying in order to make the sale. Faith bought a variety of fruits and vegetables, kobi and fresh tilapia from the market. Adwoa especially liked the bargaining that took place with the traders.

Adwoa asked Faith, "Ma, why didn't you bargain with the hawkers?"

Faith replied, "Sometimes I feel like giving them their asking price because they deserve it."

Adwoa teased, "Or maybe you have lost the hang of bargaining."

Faith agreed, "Yeah maybe I am a bit rusty at bargaining but give me time and I will become the chief bargainer."

Adwoa said doubtingly, "Yeah right!"

They laughed.

While purchasing their foodstuffs, Faith engaged the services of a pleasant "kayayei," a person who offers her services to carry purchases while you shop. The lady placed the goods in their car.

Faith asked Adwoa as they were leaving the Makola Market, "How did you like the market?"

Adwoa replied, "I like the atmosphere and most of all, the fresh fruits and vegetables, but it was too busy."

Faith worried about Adwoa's "but." There always seemed to be a "but." *Was Adwoa liking life in Accra or not?* she wondered. Faith said, "The produce comes directly from the farmers in the villages so that's why I prefer to shop at the markets. Not only is the produce fresher and cheaper, but I like to support the local farmers. They tend to use little to no synthetic fertilizers, making the produce healthier too. We had to buy organic food to get such luxury in Toronto. When I don't need to buy as much fresh food, I will get it from the hawkers closer to where we live."

From the market, Adwoa and Faith went to the supermarket to buy the remainder of items on their list. Adwoa noticed that there were similar items she could get in Toronto at the store but they weren't cheap.

Adwoa concluded, "Ma, what I find surprising is that from all the shopping we did, we ended up with just a few cans and boxes. It is very different from what we are used to. There is far less packaging. Plus without any advertising mail, we'll have less garbage now."

When they reached home, Esi, the housegirl, helped to carry the groceries from the car to the kitchen and then unpacked them.

Adwoa gasped, "Sure, we have less can and box waste but look at all of these!" Pointing to all the empty plastic bags on the counter, she declared, "They use plastic bags too much!"

"I totally agree," Faith said. "Plastic bags are used for everything, but what's worse is that people discard them everywhere. They should at least be reused."

Adwoa said, "You can even see the discarded plastic bags stuck in the ground and trapped in bushes from where the wind blows them around. Aren't we always picking up bags that blow under our main gate and over the front wall?"

"Plastic bags are harmful to the environment because they are not **biodegradable**. They often choke gutters,

25

creating breeding grounds for mosquitoes when the water can't drain properly.

"That eventually leads to flooding and to the spread of malaria. When garbage doesn't decompose quickly, it contaminates the soil and water, causing diseases like cholera," Faith added.

Adwoa exclaimed, "Malaria and cholera! They sound like awful diseases."

"Yes they are serious diseases. Some people die from them every year," Faith confirmed. "If we keep the environment clean, it would improve our health."

Adwoa suggested, "If they charged money for plastic bags it would probably deter people from using them so much."

Faith replied, "We just have to discipline ourselves. The plastic water sachets from pure water packaging and bottles, to a lesser extent, create a similar problem." Faith exclaimed, "Something really has to be done about it! They should at least use biodegradable bags more. If not, they should consider banning plastic bags altogether."

Adwoa agreed. "I know Ma. It is that serious." Adwoa asked, "Have plastic bags always been used so much?"

Faith answered, "No. For instance when I was growing up, we used rattan and straw baskets which were re-usable and we used to wrap things like yams, cassava and plantain in old newspapers. Some prepared foods were also wrapped in leaves, like banana leaves. Today even these types of goods are put in plastic bags. Even when we used plastic bags in the past, we reused them because they weren't given freely like nowadays."

"So why such a drastic change? I noticed that the salespeople automatically put the merchandise in plastic bags. I am sure that in many cases, if they weren't offered, customers would do without them," Adwoa concluded.

Faith cautioned, "Don't get me wrong. It isn't that plastic or the use of plastic is bad; it is just that it is difficult to degrade as waste. Plastic is long-lasting, durable and flexible. That's why it is so widely used. Not until we find ways to recycle or repurpose plastic a lot more, we should not use it as much as we do. We should use less of it wherever possible to protect the environment.

"You know, if our family doesn't make a conscious effort to reduce waste, after a while we could become complacent like everyone else."

This topic struck a chord with Adwoa. "Not me, Ma. I am going to help do something about waste and help to make our city clean. Somehow plastic waste seems to concern me most, even more than some of the more critical environmental issues that we have," said Adwoa earnestly. "And you know plastic waste was not our biggest issue in Canada."

Faith suggested, "Maybe finding a solution to plastic is your calling."

Then and there, Adwoa felt her attitude towards being in Ghana lifting up for the first time.

4

A Green Opportunity

Adwoa was going to be a student at Madina Heights Junior High School (JHS). It was a week before school started so she went with her parents to meet the principal and her teacher to finalize things for the start date.

After meeting with the principal, Adwoa and her parents met Mrs. Frempong, Adwoa's classroom teacher. Mrs. Frempong greeted the Mensahs warmly.

On entering the room, Mrs. Frempong said, "Hello Mr. and Mrs. Mensah. It is nice to meet you. Akwaaba!" She turned to Adwoa and said with a smile, "This must be my new student, Grace Comfort Adwoa Mensah."

Adwoa replied, "Yes Madam."

The Mensahs thanked Mrs. Frempong for her warm welcome.

After confirming that all of their concerns were addressed, Mrs. Frempong told Adwoa that she was delighted to have her in her class. She assured Adwoa that she would love attending Madina Heights JHS.

Mrs. Frempong asked, "Adwoa do you have any questions?"

Adwoa replied, "Yes Madam. Does the school have a green programme or a green group?"

Mrs. Frempong answered, "The school does not have a green programme or group. We teach environmental studies as part of our science curriculum."

Adwoa told Mrs. Frempong, "I am interested in joining a green group. In Canada, I was a member of one at my school and we did a lot of activities to help make our school green as well as participate in green projects in the community."

Mrs. Frempong commented, "That's great. We could do with lots more involvement of our youth in promoting environmental awareness and engaging in community activities."

"Madam, as you can see, Adwoa is very passionate about the environment," Faith pointed out.

"Yes, in fact I am impressed," remarked Mrs. Frempong. "I belong to a community group that is committed to building our community and improving our environmental conditions and lifestyles. Our environment is the root cause of most of our health problems. I strongly feel that educating our youth about the environment will give them a better appreciation of the threats to it and to them. It will impress upon our youth the need to protect the environment for their wellbeing.

"We couldn't have met at a better time. I am working with a team to create a green group as an extracurricular activity for junior high school students in Madina Heights. Grace, can I count on you to help with organizing the group?" said Mrs. Frempong.

"Yes Mrs. Frempong, I would love to help with organizing the group and I will be a very active member," Adwoa replied with conviction.

31

Mrs. Frempong went on to say, "We will start with a membership drive when school begins. The group will have my team's full support as well as support from community organizations and businesses."

As they left the school, Sam said to Adwoa, "You have done a great job so far, especially at home. You have increased our awareness about the environment, and it affects the choices we make. There are big challenges here in Ghana so don't get disheartened; just remember that one person can make a difference. A person can inspire others to help realize a vision. People working together can achieve great things."

Faith agreed with Sam's comments and said, "Amen!"

On their way back from Madina Heights JHS, the Mensahs stopped at a store to pick up some items that they had ordered. The route to the store required them to pass by Achimota Forest, a huge forest in the heart of Accra.

Sam pointed out, "Adwoa here you have it, a forest in the city! How do you like that?"

Adwoa said, "That's so cool! We won't have to go far to visit a forest. I am sure that they take students there on field trips regularly."

Sam replied, "Even here in the capital this forest has to be rescued from being endangered. As you can see, people have put up structures and buildings around it, some of them encroaching on the forest land."

5

Off to School

At last, it was time for the reopening of school. The long vacation and the transition to living in Ghana had ended quickly for Adwoa and Ebo.

Ebo was leaving the next day to attend secondary school at Palm Coast Senior High School, a public boarding school in Cape Coast. It was a school renowned for its quality education and it had a number of esteemed graduates who went on to become prominent members of society.

The Mensahs felt very lucky for Ebo to gain acceptance to the school. They believed that like themselves, it was better for senior high school students to attend boarding school where they could focus on schoolwork, be more disciplined and develop a sense of independence and maturity.

Back in Toronto, Ebo had attended the closest high school in the area where they lived. Unlike this, in Ghana students were assigned to schools based upon the results of the Basic Education Certificate Examination (BECE) and to one of the schools of their choice, by a Computerized School Selection and Placement System (CSSPS). Since Ebo didn't write the BECE exam, his school placement was based on his Canadian grades and available spots from the schools which his parents selected. Competition was usually fierce in securing placement at the best and most reputable schools.

They packed Ebo's school supplies, a mattress, his chop box containing food provisions and most of his personal belongings for the trip. The whole family accompanied him to move in to the boarding school.

It was a short space of time in which Adwoa would part with yet another loved one, her brother with whom she had shared her whole life and whom she adored.

Adwoa and her family left for Palm Coast Senior High School on a Saturday morning. It took about three and a half hours to reach Cape Coast where the secondary school was located. They drove through the coastal town of Kosoa, past Winneba, Apam, Mankessim and Salt Pond which had been noted historically for its salt pond and in recent years for its offshore crude oil resources.

They finally reached picturesque Cape Coast, the capital of the Central Region of Ghana.

Adwoa remarked, "Cape Coast is very beautiful. I like seeing the sea and coconut trees. If I lived here I would go to the beach often."

Sam added, "I would eat lots of fish since you could get them fresh from the sea. They have many delicious and unique seafood dishes here. As a matter of fact, once we get Ebo settled in, we will go somewhere for lunch."

"Are students allowed to go to the beach on their own?" Adwoa asked Ebo.

"Ebo replied, "I am not sure but I hope so. If we can't go alone, then at least we should be allowed to go in supervised groups. It will be terrible if we are to stay so close to beaches but cannot enjoy them."

Cape Coast was a fishing town and formerly the hub of the slave trade in West Africa. It bordered the Atlantic Ocean and its shores were lined with coconut trees and dotted with small fishing communities.

Ebo was more pensive than usual during the drive to Cape Coast. Perhaps he was thinking about starting a new school without friends, or he was thinking about the more immediate parting with loved ones so soon again. Usually this was the time that students looked forward to. It's what they would have dreamt about for so long—being away from home and living on their own. The chance to be free, independent and be with like-minded teens had finally come and for Ebo, it happened sooner than it would have if he were still in Toronto. Adwoa thought that he was nervous because she noticed he shuffled his feet a lot.

After helping Ebo to move in, the family went to look for somewhere to have lunch. They ended up at a seaside chop bar called Sandy

Shore Chop Bar. They were seated on the terrace overlooking the beach.

As they approached a table, Sam said, "This is nice!" He settled down in a chair and scouted out the surroundings.

Faith said after a sip of coconut water, "Aah, I could relax here for the rest of the day."

Ebo and Adwoa were busy checking out the menu items after which they watched the waves break and rush to shore.

Adwoa commented, "The boats are all heading in the same direction. Won't they spread out so that they can catch more fish?"

Ebo said, "Maybe they are now coming back from fishing. The fishermen must be bringing in their catch at this time so that they can sell it by the end of the day."

Sam said, "I'll see if we can buy some to take back home."

After having a delicious lunch and enjoying the scenery, the family headed back to the school dormitory, but not before stopping to buy some fresh fish.

Faith said, "Ebo, I am glad that we got to spend some extra time together at lunch."

Sam, Faith and Adwoa said their sad goodbyes to Ebo with hugs and kisses.

Faith assured Ebo, "Everything will be fine. If you need anything, please let us know. I hope that you and your roommates get on well together."

Sam said, "Be good and concentrate on your studies. Let us hear from you often."

Adwoa fought back tears while hugging Ebo and said, "We'll be in touch."

Ebo promised, "I'll be calling a lot. Talk to you later!"

Then they waved goodbye and departed.

On the way back home, Adwoa was already missing Ebo, but she tried to focus on her own start of school which was the following Monday, when her classes would actually begin. This was unlike Ebo whose classes were to start two days after Adwoa's. Adwoa felt lucky to be going to day school where she would return home every day.

When they passed a billboard that showed the direction to Cape Coast Castle, Adwoa asked, "Can we visit the castle please?"

Faith said, "It may be too late for a tour of the castle and it might even be closed."

Sam decided, "We can drive by the castle to see it anyway."

Adwoa was surprised when they drove up to the castle.

She said, "I was expecting to see an old, dark and dreary building made from stone with round towers or turrets and pointed roofs, not this massive white building nestled against the sea."

Adwoa remembered the storybooks that she read when she was younger about princesses, castles, dungeons and wicked witches, of which Snow White and the Seven Dwarfs was her favourite because of its happy ending. Unlike those old, dark, cold and dreary-looking castles in fairy tales, Cape Coast Castle looked bright, welcoming and innocent. The castle stood before them, an impressive fortress with relics of cannons pointing out to sea, seemingly to ward off attacks from the enemy in battle and to protect the townspeople.

Adwoa inquired, "Do people live in the castle or is it just a tourist attraction?"

Faith answered, "The castle has been designated a historical site. It has become a tourist attraction."

"So what's the story of Cape Coast Castle?" Adwoa quizzed.

Sam replied, "This white-washed castle, as do the many other castles in Ghana, has its own story of horror and shame but not with a happy ending."

Sam stopped the car where the castle was in full view and said, "This castle was built by Europeans. The building was used for conducting trade. Originally, the Europeans would buy goods, especially gold and mostly mahogany wood from Ghana. Ghanaian traders in turn would buy clothing, sugar, spices and other goods from the Europeans.

"Later, trading people became more profitable than trading goods. Trading people from Ghana and neighbouring countries began as there was a growing demand for cheap labour in far away countries. Most of the people that were traded were captured, shackled and crammed into holding cells at the castle. To accommodate the increasing number of captives, dungeons were added to the castle.

"The captives lived in awful and inhumane conditions at the castle until those who survived were packed into ships. The ships then set off on perilous journeys to take the captives to North America, the Caribbean and South America, mainly Brazil. The captives that survived the journey across the Atlantic Ocean were sold as slaves, most of them to work on plantations."

"That's so terrible!" Adwoa said. "Why didn't they destroy the castles when the slave trade stopped? They represent so much suffering, death and evil."

Faith replied, "The buildings are kept as historical sites—as testimonies of what happened in our past. The castles represent a gloomy part of our history and that of the descendants of the slaves. In a way, the castle is a reminder to all generations of this horrible human tragedy and for everyone to make sure that it never happens again."

Faith teased, "You have already started school, except that today's schooling is outside of the classroom. There is something new to learn every day!"

Adwoa enjoyed the scenery on the way home, especially the shades of green from natural vegetation, rock formations and fresh air in the sparsely populated countryside. Somehow Adwoa couldn't help thinking about Cape Coast Castle. She thought of the people and their lives as slaves after leaving Ghana. She wondered and tried to make sense of it.

As they approached an area where hawkers were selling foodstuffs along the roadside, Faith said to Sam, "Let's stop to buy some fruits and vegetables. They are straight from the farms and much cheaper than close to home."

They bought some plantain, pineapples, watermelon and tomatoes before continuing on to Accra where traffic was much heavier.

The Founding of a Green Group

After Ebo went away to school, Adwoa appreciated having many people around at home so she wouldn't be as lonely as she would have been otherwise. Unlike her home in Toronto where she lived together with her parents and Ebo, there were a number of other people who lived in the compound of her home in Ghana.

There was Esi, the "housegirl," who looked after housekeeping duties like cleaning, doing laundry and assisting with cooking. There was the security guard and gardener, Emmanuel, who was responsible for letting people and vehicles through the gates, sweeping the yard, attending to the gardens and washing the cars. There were two gates at the front walled fence, one for vehicles and one for people walking into the compound.

There was also Kwesi, the driver who drove Faith wherever she wanted to go, went on errands for the family and was responsible for driving Adwoa to and from school. Separate from the main house was a boy's quarters where the security guard and the housegirl lived. At the front by the gates was a small security post in which the security guard worked.

On the first day of school, Adwoa hung up her neatly-pressed uniform and had her socks and her polished shoes set aside. Her books and school supplies were already packed. The only thing left to do was to get dressed and pack her lunch into her backpack. Adwoa liked that she'd be going to a private school where she could wear her hair in different styles rather than the mandatory low afro worn by students who attended public schools.

Adwoa was a bit nervous at first but the warm welcome from teachers and fellow students made her feel comfortable at school. Although the official language for teaching was English, Twi was the most commonly spoken language on the playground. To help Adwoa in mastering Twi, she was challenged to speak with everyone at home in Twi.

Getting members for the green group was conducted during the first three weeks of school. Adwoa was happy to participate in the membership drive along with some of her peers and with the help of Mrs. Frempong. They first advertised for group members at the four local junior high schools. It was slow at first, so they posted flyers at the community centre, churches and mosques, and advertised through social media and by word of mouth. This boosted their numbers and by the end, forty-five students had registered to become members of the green group.

At the group's first meeting, Mrs. Frempong addressed the students, "First I must thank those of you who worked so hard in getting students to sign up for this group. Secondly, I would like to thank all of you for signing up to become members of this group and for coming to the meeting today. Welcome!

"Please let me introduce you to my assistant, Mr. Boateng who is also a teacher. Those of you who attend the school where he teaches already know him. He is very interested in environmental issues and has worked on many environmental projects. And, oh yes, I should introduce myself to you as well. My name is Mrs. Frempong and I teach at Madina Heights JHS. I am also a member of an organization that works on building communities by creating and strengthen-ing community services and institutions. We provide care for the poor and needy and focus on improving the environment.

"I am dedicated to improving our environ-ment and I believe that everyone has a responsibility to preserve and protect it. Hence, I feel the need to engage our youth to do their part. My role in this group alongside Mr. Boateng is to oversee the affairs of the group since you are minors. We will be responsible for representing the group when interacting formally with outside organizations, overseeing the group's activities and ensuring the safety of its members.

"What we would like to do first today is to take attendance. After that, we would like to have an open discussion about what we hope to achieve as a group and what each of you individually would like to get out of the group. This would shed some light on your reasons for wanting to join the group. After the discussion period and getting to meet other members, we will select a name for the group and then elect and appoint the leadership of the group. If we have time afterwards, we can discuss the group's mission and vision."

There were fifty-two members present. The members had a variety of reasons for joining the group: from being led by their parents to do so or just wanting something to do, to having a keen interest and commitment in helping to protect the environment. Generally, members wanted to improve the state of communities by keeping them clean from garbage, creating green spaces and helping to protect natural resources.

Members felt that there should be more groups that were similar across the country and at senior high schools, colleges and universities. They believed that their participation could make a positive difference to the environment.

Members settled on "Madina Heights Environmental Stewards" (MHES) as the name of the group. They elected Kofi as president, Mohammed as vice president, and Wisdom as secretary. Adwoa was elected Fundraising Coordinator. This meant that she was responsible for finding ways to get money so the group could pay for things with their funds. Adwoa was hoping to utilize her past experience in fundraising in her new role.

The group agreed that meetings would be held twice a month on Saturdays from 9:00 a.m. at the community centre. The meetings were scheduled to last for one and a half hours. Meetings would not be held during the Christmas or Easter breaks but would continue for a month after the school year when students would be on vacation and had more time to devote to the group's activities.

The group later agreed on their mission statement and vision. The MHES mission was: *to promote environmental awareness and education so that caring for the environment became second nature.*

MHES's vision was: *improved environmental standards resulting in good sanitation, a continuous supply of electricity and clean water, and the protection of Ghana's natural resources.*

Members of each of the four junior high schools in Madina Heights that were part of the group were tasked with finding ways to make their individual schools greener. Three of the schools were public schools and one was a private school. MHES planned to organize at least one community activity each school year.

Galamsey

Ghana was once called the Gold Coast. It was rich in minerals, especially gold, aluminum, diamonds and bauxite. MHES was asked to participate in a project to plant trees in a badly damaged forest near a small village called Awaso. Some digging had been allowed on the grounds of the forest to mine for gold and precious stones in the past, but many foreigners had come in search of gold to improve their fortunes and were breaking the law. Some local people also did this. This illegal mining was called "**galamsey.**"

Galamsey operators often displaced the local communities by damaging their farms and contaminating their water bodies, leaving them without the normal means to earn their livelihoods. The galamseyers occasionally scared off local people with weapons and threats of violence. They often avoided detection from government and local officials but in many instances they colluded with them secretly.

The forest for the MHES project was called Samandua Forest. It was very badly damaged by the galamseyers who used heavy machinery to excavate the land to mine gold. The illegal miners dug up the land in the forest and other nearby protected areas. They dug many illegal mines and diverted water from the nearby Tano River to use in the process of extracting gold.

Galamseyers left the water and soil contaminated with traces of mercury, cyanide and other toxic chemicals, making it harmful for growing crops and fishing. They chopped down trees to clear the ground to make way for their mining activities, leaving the once vibrant forest and ecosystems badly damaged. This left the poor farming community near Samandua Forest deva-stated and with contaminated water as their only source of **potable** water.

MHES accepted the invitation to participate in the project from an organization called "Trees for Life." Trees for Life was a non-profit organization which was committed to planting trees around the world to achieve its goal of improving Earth's environment. The trees would be identified so that each student would always know which tree he or she planted and adopted. It was felt that if the youth had a vested interest in the forest, they would be more likely to help protect the forest in the future. They would have a sense of ownership and pride of the trees.

All MHES members participated in the reforestation project. The students were excited about going on the field trip. Before the trip, MHES had a meeting at which members were given more information about the project and the trip. They were told that it took about seven and a half hours to reach Samandua Forest from Madina Heights. The route that was planned for getting to the forest was to travel along Ghana's southern coast to Takoradi and then north past Awaso to Samandua Forest.

On the way back they would take a different route. From Samandua Forest, they would travel south for a short distance to Awaso, then head eastward to Kumasi, the capital of the Ashanti Region, and continue southeast to Koforidua, the capital of the Eastern Region. They would continue to travel south from Koforidua back to Madina Heights. It would be a long journey.

Members were shown the location of the forest on a map and they were briefed about the Western Region and its importance to Ghana. The students learned that the majority of the region, which was located in Ghana's forest zone, was made up of rainforests, coastal wetlands and mangroves. Sekondi-Takoradi was the twin city capital and hub of the Western Region. A great part of environmental damage in the region was caused by deforestation due to excessive and uncontrolled logging of timber and farming. These activities contributed to a loss of biodiversity, soil erosion, **desertification** and ultimately climate change.

The region was the home of several forest reserves and national parks such as Subri River Forest Reserve, Cape Three Points National Park, Bia Reserve and Opon Mansi Forest Reserve.

One of the awful results of galamsey activity was that it left the land so bare and ruined that it stole from Ghana all the wonderful ways in which forests can bring riches to a country. In other words, it made poverty worse.

It would take about seven and a half hours to drive each way to reach Samandua Forest from Madina Heights and return, after allowing for planned stops, traffic and road conditions. Due to the distance and travel time, the group would camp overnight at a site near the forest.

8

On the Way to Samandua Forest

Around 6:00 a.m. the following Saturday morning, a caravan of two buses and four mini vans carrying the students, team leaders, teachers and some parents, left for Samandua Forest. From Madina Heights, the caravan drove through the crowded metropolis of Greater Accra, with its collection of luxurious mansions, comfortable dwellings and squatters' shacks. Along the route, many traders sold mangoes, pineapples, watermelons, peppers, tomatoes, cassava, yams, plantain, gari and charcoal. A few hawkers displayed "grass cutters," a bush meat which is considered a local delicacy.

The caravan journeyed through the urban sprawl of the Greater Accra Region, westward through the Central Region and towards Takoradi, the capital of the Western Region. They stopped for a break for forty-five minutes in Takoradi after which they headed north through the lush countryside. They passed by many isolated small towns and villages with dilapidated houses and clusters of mud huts with thatched roofs. The convoy travelled past cocoa plantations and mango orchards as well as banana and plantain groves.

The caravan continued north and farther into the countryside where road conditions deteriorated because of bumpy dirt roads. They drove near Tana Suraw Forest Reserve amidst endless trees in the heart of forestland. Everywhere outside was green except for the road and sky. The fertile land and normal rainy conditions enabled the trees to tower above each other to compete for direct sunlight and created an enormous canopy. At the edge of the road, thick brush fenced the forest, shielding the wildlife within. It was mid November when the long dry season had begun to set in. The moisture from the rainy season was diminishing, leaving the air warm but humid.

At least two adults travelled on each bus. Mrs. Frempong rode on the bus that Adwoa travelled in. When they reached about two kilometers away from Samandua Forest, Mrs. Frempong pointed out some huge and very tall trees that dwarfed the other trees around them.

She said, "Those huge trees are native to this area. They are usually found in the interior of forests and tend to have shrub growing beneath them. The trees are called "forbidden" trees and their fruit are called "ghost fruit."

There was a flood of questions from curious students.

"Is that what ghosts eat?"

"Are there ghosts in the forest?"

"Why are they called forbidden trees?"

Mrs. Frempong explained, "The legend says that it is called the forbidden tree because of its fruit. They say that if you touch or use the small berries, a curse will befall you."

Adwoa looked around at other students with a smirk, half considering it could be true, half in disbelief. She decided, as she lowered her eyes, to dismiss the idea as a silly, old wives' tale.

They finally reached their destination, an area at the northeast side of Samandua Forest. Already gathered at the entrance to the site were some local residents who came to the forest to support the students and participate in the event. When the caravan arrived, the onlookers cheered and gave the members of MHES a hearty welcome.

Mrs. Frempong told the students, "Straight ahead of us you will see huge craters. Beside them are piles of dirt and no trees. That's the damage caused by the galamseyers and it is the reason why we are here. Planting new trees will bring new life to the forest."

The students were dismayed to see the havoc created by the excavation of the land by galamseyers. The galamseyers had destroyed a large area of trees and other vegetation. The ground was mucky and they had left behind tools and open pits as they moved on to other areas in the forests in search of gold. *How could anyone come to a place green and thriving with life and leave it this way after they were done with it?* Adwoa thought. The devastation of the forest and damage to the environment was contrary to

MHES' mission and its goals to protect Ghana's resources.

The place where the trees were destroyed was hidden in an area deep into the forest. The drivers tried to take the buses as close as possible to the area. When they reached as far as the vehicles could go, everyone got out and walked a fair distance along a narrow, rough and winding path. The path led to a big open space in the forest.

Although most of the felled trees were already cleared from the area, some rotten trees and branches were left behind. There were plans to remove the remaining branches to reduce chances of a forest fire. Some of the villagers were given the dried-up branches to use as firewood.

At the site, most of the craters were already refilled to make way for replanting of the trees. Mrs. Frempong pointed out, "The galamseyers did not refill many of the craters that they dug out, leaving them to catch water and attract mosquitoes or for people to fall into them." She cautioned the students, "Please be careful and pay attention to where you are going. Please follow the lead."

She continued, "To our right, past the bushes is the Tano River. The river used to pass along here, but over the years because of mining activities, it has been diverted and it is now contaminated. For generations it has been the only source of drinking water for the people of this small community, but things have changed. The water is no longer safe for drinking. The river is also where many of them earn their livelihood from fishing."

Adwoa asked, "So where do the people get clean water for their families and animals from?"

Mrs. Frempong replied, "Water is scarce, not only because of contamination of the river but also due to less rainfall, and this is happening throughout the country. Less rainfall is due, in part, to the destruction of our forests. It's all connected. During the rainy season it isn't as bad because water collects in ponds and wells and the people also collect rainwater for their own household needs while the rains wet their farms. It is the dry season that is hardest because that's when the river has less water.

In recent years, the river has been drying up in some areas. This small community is virtually cut off from the other villages and because they don't have other sources of potable water, sometimes they have little choice other than to use the polluted water from the river."

Kofi said, "Since there is no tap water in the village and the river is polluted, it means that the only alternative source of potable water for the people would be to buy pure water, but most of them can't afford it."

Adwoa added, "That would also create more plastic waste to get rid of. Maybe they could dig some boreholes to get water."

Mrs. Frempong pointed out, "Sometimes it is a matter of settling for a good choice rather than the best choice. Although sachets and bottles contribute to the waste problem, it is a much better and less costly source of water than if people drank unclean water which causes all kinds of health problems and even death. Sachet water is the most affordable and available source of clean water so that's why it is so widely used. Even though it is costly, digging a few more boreholes would help solve the water problem in the long run, but again much of the soil is also polluted from mining. In a worst-case situation, the people would have to get water from Awaso."

The tree-planting ceremony began with the subchief and local government officials giving short speeches. A local dance group performed a ceremonial dance to everyone's delight. During the ceremony, they poured libation in honour of their ancestors and invoked their blessings on the forest and the project that they were embarking on.

Mrs. Frempong announced, "Today, each member of MHES will help to rebuild Samandua Forest by planting an adopted tree with pride. Each tree is a symbol of your investment in your future, in Ghana's resources and her environment. It will take about forty years for these seedlings to grow into mature trees like the ones around here. Compare that to the few minutes that it took to cut down one of these trees with a chainsaw."

Each seedling was tagged and everyone present planted one and was given its identification number.

A student asked, "What will happen to the rest of the space where we haven't planted trees?"

Mr. Boateng answered, "We are the first people to replant trees in this forest. Other students will also plant trees here and at other places where the problem exists."

The students had a sense of pride and accomplishment and pledged to remember the trees and help in any way they could to ensure that the trees survived. The teachers took the opportunity to show the students the different types of vegetation that grew in the forest. They told the students that bats lived in the forest as well as deer, guinea fowls and many different kinds of birds. They said that these species of animals and plants needed to be protected from becoming endangered. The planting of new trees would help.

9
The
Forest Keepers

As the students headed back to the area where the buses and other vehicles were parked, they scoured the ground for bits of gold. They were careful not to touch any ghost fruit. Adwoa's friend Nii Isaac said with disappointment, "The miners didn't even leave a trace of gold behind."

"I wish I could be lucky enough to find a big gold nugget. I would be rich," her friend Charity said. "But look at these beautiful stones. Aren't they pretty?" Charity asked as she held an array of shiny stones in her open palms.

Other students admired the stones and started to gather some too. They were the type of stones that were usually polished and used for making jewellery.

Adwoa secretly wished that she could stumble upon a nugget of gold. As she reached closer to the bus, she thought that she caught a glimpse of something shiny on the ground beneath some shrubs. She stopped and took a step backward, but didn't see anything shiny. Adwoa moved forward and again she saw something on the ground glimmer. As she went closer, the object continued to shine in the sunlight. Adwoa felt a gush of excitement but restrained herself from declaring her luck until she got hold of what could be her new-found treasure.

The shiny object rested between two ghost fruit on the ground. It seemed to beckon to her. Adwoa couldn't remove the shiny object without touching the ghost fruit but she couldn't resist trying to pick up the object. Lots of the berries from forbidden trees were scattered under the trees and they looked ordinary and harmless.

Charity noticed that Adwoa was distracted and was lagging behind. She said, "What are you doing? Come on!"

Adwoa said, "Wait a minute." She fetched a plastic cup from her backpack, skillfully tip-toed between the scattered ghost fruit and carefully maneuvered the cup and its cover to scoop the two fruit and the shiny object into it. Then Adwoa shuffled the contents of the cup around until she was able to separate the nugget from the fruit. She poured the shiny object from the cup and inspected it to see if it was really a gold nugget. Adwoa then covered the cup with its lid and put it in her backpack.

Adwoa and her friends examined her find that contained a shiny portion caked with dirt and rocks. They were bubbling with excitement as she pried away the rocky encasement.

"It's gold. This is my lucky day!" Adwoa exclaimed.

"You are so lucky," Charity told her. "You are the only one of us to find gold. If we had more time, maybe some more of us could find nuggets or even grains of gold."

"What are you going to do with the gold nugget?" Nii Isaac asked.

"I'll show it to my parents and see what they say," Adwoa replied.

Charity said, "If it were mine, I would ask my parents to take it to a jeweller to see how much it is worth."

Adwoa said, "Since it isn't that big, I might keep it as a lucky charm or get a pendant made out of it."

The students boarded the buses and the caravan drove a short distance to the site where they were going to camp for the night. The camp was in an open area in forestland. It was early evening and the tents were already set up and ready for them to move in. The adults started right away preparing to serve the food that they brought for everyone to eat. Almost all of the students had never gone camping before so they were enjoying the new experience.

In a short space of time, the sun escaped behind the tall trees leaving the areas around the campsite in total darkness. After dinner, everyone gathered in a group outside the tent area. They discussed the events of the day and talked about what they would be doing the next day when they planned to head back home. They sang songs and the teachers told them interesting folklore including Anansi stories.

It was finally time for the students to settle down to sleep. They had listened to wonderful tales outside while admiring stars in a moonless sky and watched fireflies dart in the air like meandering specs of light. The chatter and excitement died down as everyone fell asleep, except the three security guards stationed outside the tent area.

As Adwoa tried to fall asleep, she thought of her family back home and all the things that she had seen on the trip: the beaches on the Atlantic Ocean, fishing villages, bustling towns, waterfalls, swamps and endless trees and bushes of a wide botanical diversity. She had seen many people along the way, city people and rural people alike, but she hadn't seen many animals except for birds, of which the Western Region had a rich variety of species.

She saw all kinds of butterflies of different sizes and colours. They were beautiful beyond words. When Adwoa was in the forest earlier, she saw movement in the bushes at times but didn't see any animals. She thought that the animals could have been monkeys or chimpanzees which were native to the Western Region.

The silence of the night was broken by the chirping of countless crickets and from the sounds of unidentified nocturnal animals which did not give the silent trees any rest. *What if the ghosts are roaming in the forest?*, Adwoa feared. She then thought of the destruction that she had seen in the forest and couldn't understand why it couldn't be stopped.

Her thoughts drifted to the local village people, wondering about their everyday lives, especially children like herself. She thought of how close to the riches of the land the villagers were, yet how poor they remained. Maybe some of them were small-scale miners trying to make a living from mining without the proper equipment. She wished that the villagers could all become rich from the land some day.

Heading
Back Home

The next morning everyone was up bright and early. The temperature was cool overnight and it was misty early in the morning. The mist gradually cleared as the sun rose.

While they were having breakfast together, Mrs. Frempong reminded everyone, "Our plan for today is to drive back to Madina Heights. It will take just as long as when we came, roughly seven and a half hours. We are going to travel further inland via the major route from Awaso and drive northeast through the Ashanti Region to Kumasi, its capital. We will stop for lunch at Juaso in the Ashanti Region and then continue through the Eastern Region on to the Greater Accra Region."

Mrs. Frempong briefed the students about the Ashanti Region. She told them that like the

Western Region, the majority of people who lived in the Ashanti kingdom were Akans. She shared that the head or king of the kingdom was called the "Asantehene." Adwoa took special interest in travelling through these regions because her mother was Fante and her father was Ashanti. Both were part of the Akan tribe.

They boarded the buses and the caravan drove past a section of the Tano River. Adwoa said, "Look how muddy the water is. How can people ever drink that water without getting sick?"

Mrs. Frempong said, "It is not just mud that gives it that colour. It is all the contaminants in it too." She pointed out, "Look way over there at the riverbank and you will see some mining equipment and illegal miners busy at work."

Kofi asked, "Are many other rivers polluted like this?"

Mrs. Frempong replied, "Several of our rivers are contaminated. Some of them are the Pra, Daboase and Ankobra. They are here in the Western Region and there are the Birim and Densu rivers too. That's quite a lot and many of them like the Pra River, pass through large areas. The Pra River ends up in the Ivory Coast next door. Water pollution is a very big problem in Ghana."

A student asked, "So why isn't anything being done to stop it before there is no clean water left anywhere in Ghana?"

Mrs. Frempong replied, "The solution seems simple but there are a lot of parties involved so not until Ghanaians and our leaders take the problem seriously and do something about it, will things change, I am afraid."

As the caravan entered the Ashanti Region, it passed signs leading to operations of some international companies who were mining manganese and gold. In just over two and a half hours they reached Kumasi, the busy city which was already crowded. The caravan stopped for a lunch break at Juaso.

When they were having lunch, Nii Isaac asked Adwoa, "What will you do with the ghost fruit that you brought with you?"

Adwoa answered, "I'll probably just keep them for a while to see if anything happens. I know they will just rot."

Nii Isaac asked, "What if the story about the curse is true? Aren't you afraid that something could happen to you?"

"Something like what? They are just fruit and I am not going to touch them or use them. If the tree and fruit had any powers, they wouldn't have allowed galamseyers to destroy the forest," Adwoa reasoned.

"Maybe the forbidden tree put a curse on the forest and that's why part of it was destroyed," Nii Isaac argued.

Adwoa said logically, "Then it would have caused its own destruction. Some forbidden trees were cut down too. I don't believe that a tree or fruit can cause a curse at all," she continued defensively, "Maybe the legend isn't true. What if it's a good curse, a blessing?"

"A good curse! Who ever heard of a good curse?" Nii Isaac objected.

"Well there are opposites in everything," Adwoa guessed.

Adwoa went on to tell Nii Isaac about a dream that she had the night before. She told him, "In my dream the villagers woke up one morning to find ghost fruit scattered everywhere outside their huts. At first they thought that it was a bad omen and they were afraid, even to go outside. Then the local spiritualist told them not to be afraid and that the ghost fruit was a good omen. When the spiritualist examined the ghost fruit closely, he found that they were made of pure gold. Everyone began rejoicing and could not believe their good luck. All the village people became very rich."

Nii Isaac replied, "Well let's hope that yours bring you good luck and riches too!"

They continued on their journey and drove southeast into the Eastern Region. In the Eastern Region, most of the inhabitants were also Akans. The terrain was different from the Central, Western and Ashanti Regions where they had travelled during the trip. The land and roadways were hilly. They continued to travel south through Koforidua.

Mrs. Frempong pointed out the Krobo Mountains and Akwapim Ridge in the distance. She told the students, "You will notice that there are also a lot of forested areas in the Eastern Region and because of its high landscape, there are many waterfalls. In the eastern part of the region which is to our left, is the Volta River and Lake Volta, the largest man-made lake on earth. That is where the Akosombo Dam which produces hydroelectric power for the country is located."

Adwoa asked, "Will we be going to see the dam?"

Mrs. Frempong replied, "I'm afraid not. There is so much to see there that it would take a separate trip just to visit the dam and nearby attractions. We don't have time to go there today."

They continued to travel south, past Aburi Botanical Gardens with which most of the students were familiar. It wasn't long before they reached Madina Heights.

Lucky or Not

Adwoa told her friends in Toronto about the field trip to Samandua Forest and about her treasure. She sent them pictures too. They were disgusted at the damage to the forest but were somewhat intrigued at the notion of gold prospecting. They offered suggestions as to what Adwoa should do with the gold nugget.

One afternoon when Adwoa talked to her friend Shawn in Toronto, the topic of the weather came up. Shawn asked, "So what season are you in now?"

Adwoa explained, "The rainy season here is ending. The hot, dry season is on its way."

He asked, "What is the rainy season like?"

Adwoa replied, "There are frequent showers and torrential rains. To me, in Ghana the clouds, sky and sun always seem nearer than in Canada. One night we had an awful rainstorm. It was as though the sky had burst open and poured pellets on the ground. The thunder roared and rolled across the lowered sky while lightning lit up everything. Gosh! I was so scared. You would think that Mother Nature was angry."

Shawn replied, "I could just imagine it. So was there a lot of flooding since you said that the gutters are sometimes clogged?"

Adwoa told him, "Yes, as usual. Although people are familiar with the rainy season, they seemed to be quite unprepared for the flooding that occurred in the low-lying parts of the city. Lots of homes and properties were damaged this year. By the next morning after the storm, it was very calm outside; it was like an angelic kid after throwing a temper tantrum. Apart from the inconvenient rains and pesky mosquitoes, the rainy season was pleasant, as it was cooler and more comfortable." Adwoa asked, "How was fall?"

Shawn replied, "Fall was beautiful as usual. You know that it is one of my favourite seasons because of the colourful leaves and cool temperatures. Now I have to brace myself for winter. I hope that we will have a good one this year."

Adwoa said, "I hope that winter won't be too bad for you; at least that there won't be too much snow. While you are having extreme cold, I'll be having extreme heat because it will be the dry season called Harmattan. I'll let you know what it's like."

After considering the recommendations from friends along with her own wishes, Adwoa decided she would get a pendant made from the gold nugget that she found in Samandua Forest. She dreamt of how beautiful the pendant would be. She thought of having it designed in the shape of a butterfly, her favourite insect, but felt that the nugget might not be big enough to make one. Otherwise she would settle for a heart or a cross.

She pictured how lovely it would look on her gold chain. The pendant would rest just at her neckline where it could be easily seen and admired. It would forever remind her of her first strike of good fortune—the first of many to come, she hoped. First she wanted to find out the value of the nugget and determine how much it would cost to get the pendant made.

One day she asked Sam, "Dad, can you please take me to the jewellers when you go to town tomorrow?"

"Why do you want to go the jewellers?" Sam asked.

"To find out how much my gold nugget is worth?" Adwoa replied.

"Your gold nugget?" he asked.

"Yes, the one that I found in Samandua Forest. Remember?" Adwoa answered, wondering why her dad would forget the nugget after she had made such a fuss about finding it.

"Is it really yours?" he asked.

Adwoa was even more confused. She said, "Yes, it is mine."

"Anyway, you can come with me tomorrow. I'll be leaving around noon," Sam said.

Adwoa later recounted the incident to her brother Ebo. She asked, "Why would Dad ask if the nugget was mine when he knew that I found it?"

"Why didn't you ask him? Maybe he wants you to think about it—to figure it out for yourself." Ebo said.

"What do you mean? Figure what out?" Adwoa asked.

"It is not a clear-cut situation, but you will have to let your conscience guide you. You see, you found the nugget which was left behind by the galamseyers who were stealing it from the forest because they dug it up illegally. So the question is, who does the nugget really belong to?" Ebo pointed out.

"Oh! I never thought of it that way," Adwoa confessed. "So what do you think I should do with it?" she asked with reluctance and some disappointment.

"It's all up to you. You must advise yourself and decide what to do," Ebo told her.

Adwoa thought long and hard about who rightfully owned the gold nugget and what to do with it. She figured that she had no way of knowing who the galamseyer was that mined the nugget. She wondered, *If it is not the galamseyer's gold nugget nor mine, and if I shouldn't bury it back in the forest, does it belong to the chief of the area or the government? What about "finders keepers"?*

A few days passed and then weeks, but nothing happened to the ghost fruit in the plastic cup. Just as Adwoa expected, the fruit eventually started to change colour and decay. One day Adwoa cleared stuff from her desk, including the cup of ghost fruit, to make room for a school project that she was working on. She placed the cup of fruit on the bookcase in her room and forgot about it.

Some time later, Nii Isaac asked, "Whatever happened to the ghost fruit?"

Adwoa admitted, "I haven't checked on them in a while, but there's no curse. Nothing bad has happened."

Nii Isaac conceded, "I guess you were right after all. As for legends, who knows the true stories behind them?"

That evening, Adwoa decided to check out the cup of fruit. She removed the clutter from the bookshelf but didn't see the cup. She looked elsewhere on the bookshelf and in her room but she still couldn't find the cup. One thing was for sure, she hadn't removed it from her room.

It was time to settle down and prepare for her upcoming end-of-term tests. Adwoa decided that working on MHES's projects would have to be put on hold. Adwoa had done well in all her subjects so far, although she thought that schoolwork in Ghana would be easy for her. She was mistaken. School at Madina Heights had a different style of teaching, one that she had to get used to; it was more theoretical than practical. Coming from abroad, the expectation for her was high and she didn't want to disappoint anyone, most of all herself.

The first test was a science test. Science was one of Adwoa's favourite subjects and she always did great in it so she hadn't prepared well ahead of time. It was the evening before the test. Adwoa sat in the verandah of her home and attempted to study but she didn't accomplish much.

As time slipped away, Adwoa sat at the dining table. She readied herself to study and then leafed through her thirty pages of notes. She winced. *This is going to be a long night.* She took another sip of her ice-cold water. *Last sip before I start*, she convinced herself.

I can do this in one hour she resolved. Another sip and her eyes moved towards the first page of her notes with reluctance: the same sort of reluctance a mountain climber about to ascend the last and highest peak would have. She knew it would be great once she got through her mountain of notes, but she didn't look forward to the effort that it begged.

Finally, she began to read, "Mixtures can be classified into different types…" All of a sudden there was silence: silence and darkness. It had happened again: dumsor dumsor. Adwoa didn't pay much attention to it because she knew that in a moment, the system would switch over to the back-up generator. She waited to hear its familiar humming sound, a noise that she would prefer not to endure while studying. But having a noisy source of bright light was better than any dim, sleepy substitutes.

Like clockwork, she heard the sound of a generator kick in. She thought, *It must have read my mind and decided to please me,* because the generator was quieter than usual. It was more of a buzzing sound than a humming one, but it was still dark inside her house. Adwoa went to the window to check, only to find out that the noise was coming from her neighbour's generator, not theirs. Adwoa was in a dilemma. *How can I study at night without any light?*

Esi, the housegirl, quickly brought some solar lanterns and Sam and Faith scrambled to help light some candles. The generator wasn't working. It had either broken down or ran out of fuel. Adwoa hastily studied with dull lighting and was lucky to be able to use her laptop which was still charged. She hardly slept and woke up early in the morning, scrambling to squeeze more study time in before school started. Adwoa vowed never to be outwitted by dumsor again. She also promised herself not to wait till the last minute to study.

Still Getting Adjusted

Adwoa was faced with many challenges during her first school term. Although she liked Madina Heights JHS, she was affected by her inability to speak Twi. Adwoa was fine during class time when English was spoken, but her difficulty with Twi surfaced during recess when it was the language mostly spoken. She understood Twi far more than she could speak it. For a while, Adwoa didn't have the confidence to try to speak it for fear of making mistakes that she could later be teased about.

Adwoa found the school environment more rigid than what she was accustomed to, but she quickly adjusted to it. She and two of her classmates, Chi Chi and Precious, along with Charity and Nii Isaac, became close friends. With her friends' help and reinforcement from home, Adwoa's oral Twi began getting a lot better.

Surprisingly, Adwoa missed walking to school with her friends, which she did in Toronto. During those walks to and from school, she and her friends would spend special time together. She had enjoyed walking through the neighbourhood. When Adwoa was driven to and from school in Ghana, the only time that she could spend with her friends was at recess.

Despite having mixed feelings in the beginning about wearing uniforms to school, Adwoa began to like it because she didn't have to worry every day about what outfit and accessories to wear.

The language barrier wasn't quite the same for Ebo. He hadn't forgotten Twi; with just a little brushing up, he became fluent in the language again. However, he found the school system unbearable. Integration for him was tough. He missed home a lot and likened his school to a boot camp.

Ebo complained that students' rights were ignored and students were discouraged from questioning things. School life was too regimented for him. He hated having to do housekeeping duties and to be at the mercy of prefects and senior students. Ebo feared he was losing his cherished independence.

Ebo had always excelled in school and was usually laid back. His change in attitude was surprising. Ebo was becoming rebellious. Sam and Faith thought that Ebo's problems were due to the short timeframe between moving from Canada to attending boarding school. He was miserable but soon fate would rescue him, though at a price.

One day Ebo showed up at home with little notice. He said, "I felt as though I was catching a cold. I remembered playing in the rain the day before when our team was finishing a game of soccer. I shrugged it off at the time but I knew that getting wet after playing in the hot sun was a combination that could bring on a cold. I figured that sucking on a few mints and taking medicine would ward off the headache and slight fever that I was beginning to have.

"I felt worse as time went by, but I couldn't afford to miss classes and didn't look forward to staying alone in the dormitory. After a while, I felt that the home remedies and treatments weren't working and that I was actually getting worse. Apart from the persistent fever, I started to get chills and to feel nauseous. Then I thought that it was the stomach flu. I was also feeling weak and wanted desperately to rest in bed. I even lost my appetite and only drank fluids.

"Many of my classmates suggested that it could be malaria rather than the flu. I dreaded the possibility of contracting malaria. I reported my condition to the head prefect and he told the school matron who recommended that I see a doctor. The doctor confirmed that I was suffering from malaria. The doctor said that since I was no longer taking medication against malaria like I did when I first arrived from Canada, I was "at risk." I had thought that enough time had elapsed for me to become **acclimatized**, although I was still careful with what I consumed. The doctor said that I should go home for a week and a half to recuperate, so here I am."

Adwoa said, "Sorry Bro, but I am glad to have you back home anyway. I hope that I don't ever get sick with malaria." She giggled and teased. "See! You are so popular that even the mosquitoes are after you."

"Yeah, right! The mosquitoes should just leave me alone." Ebo said and asked, "So how are things going with you?"

Adwoa replied, "Things are going good. I have a lot to keep me busy. Apart from school and the MHES group, you know I swim and as usual, I attend church and Sunday school. I will be starting piano lessons next week too."

She asked Ebo, "Are things getting any better with you at school?"

Ebo replied, "It is becoming bearable. I am getting used to it, I guess. I still can't stand how the senior students treat the junior students. They have too much power. However, I am getting used to the style of teaching and now I know more people. I have also made a few good friends so things at school are improving."

"I am glad that you are feeling better about school," Adwoa replied. "Have you been hearing from your friends in Toronto?"

Ebo answered, "I hear from John regularly, but only now and then from the others. Most of them have part-time jobs and they are also busy doing the mandatory community work needed to graduate."

"I'm in touch with my friends there at least once a week. At first I used to communicate with at least one of them practically every day," Adwoa said.

"You and your friends always have a lot to talk about," Ebo remarked.

"Have you noticed what I have been telling you about Ma and Dad?" Adwoa asked. She went on to say, "Now that there are more people for Ma to check on, she is always on high alert and doesn't miss anything. As for Dad, the radio has become his best friend. He is now into politics more than ever and he listens to call-in shows a lot. I am sure that you have heard him commenting and arguing with what the host and callers say. It's even worse than the discussions he and his friends used to have back in Toronto.

"On top of that, Ma and Dad are very busy attending outdoorings, funerals and other functions or entertaining guests, almost every weekend. You can hardly find free time with them," Adwoa complained.

Ebo commented, "They are happier now that they are among their old friends and family and fully participating in the culture. It's what they are used to. They surely won't get bored or lonely here. For you and me, it will take time."

Adwoa started, "I think I'm beginning to find my place here." She paused, "Well, we'll see…enough about that anyways."

Before a week and a half was up, Ebo was ready to return to school, to Faith and Sam's surprise, even though he hadn't fully recovered. He didn't want to miss too many of his classes and maybe he discovered that he liked school more than he thought. It was only the home-cooked meals that tempted him to stay the full time. He made sure to take some food with him when he left.

It was then December which was approaching the end of the first school term and the start of Christmas vacation. It was also the onset of Harmattan, the worsening hot, dry season in which the Sahara Desert, with the help of **trade winds**, claimed lands to its south and west. This continuing desertification of lands in sub-Saharan Africa by the spreading of the

Sahara's sand and dust made the weather unbearable sometimes. Its reach stretched as far as the Gulf of Guinea.

During Harmattan, which started from late November and would last till mid-March, the deterioration in air quality caused Adwoa to experience asthma-like symptoms that limited her outdoor activities. She sometimes wore a surgical mask to filter the air she breathed and to avoid asthma attacks. At the official start of the dry season, the air was already hot and dry. The trade winds filled the air with dust that blocked out the sun's rays. It left one's skin dry and parched and made visibility poor. Dust seeped through every nook and cranny.

The dry air and dust, coupled with the sweltering heat, reminded Adwoa of some long, hot summer days of suffocating humidity in Toronto. The inescapable heat during the short days of Harmattan caused Adwoa's body to transpire like a leaf by magically awakening its dormant pores.

At that time, she imagined Torontonians bundled up in layers of thick clothing to keep themselves warm and to protect against frostbite.

Adwoa wasn't sure which she preferred: the heat or the cold. As if in a mirage, she wanted to trade grains of sand and particles of dust for winter's soft and fluffy snowflakes which cooled the air and melted on contact with the warm earth. It soothed her body to substitute snow banks for sand dunes.

During the dry season, Adwoa stayed indoors more and enjoyed the comfort of air condition. She noted that whether trying to escape from the heat or cold, there was a dependence on energy in the form of electricity generated from **fossil fuels** or **renewable energy**. She knew that the choice of energy used, had a direct effect on pollution and the environment.

Preparing
for Cleanup Day

It was another MHES meeting day. Mrs. Frempong informed the group, "MHES's first community activity will be to participate in a massive clean up to coincide with the monthly National Sanitation Day. By choosing to do the clean up on this particular day, the first Saturday of the month, MHES was endorsing the national cleanup exercise.

"It will generate more interest and encourage people to participate in the national campaign. The leadership of our group will meet briefly after this meeting to plan for the event which should take place in a couple of months."

Mrs. Frempong gave the group details of the planned clean up. She told Adwoa, "The responsibility of fundraising for the event will be yours. It will let you get a feel for fundraising in

Ghana as we have major fundraising goals for our group's first year. Funds will be needed to buy the gear, tools and supplies for the cleanup and to buy bins to be deposited at certain locations within the community. I will let you know what funding and donations we already expect from some of our supporters."

Mrs. Frempong informed them, "We will give you slips to get permissions from your parents to allow you to participate in the event. Mr. Boateng and I will work on getting permission from the mayor's office to allow us to go to some of the places we want to clean. We will try to get as much corporate donations of tools, gear and safety equipment as possible."

Kofi, the president, asked, "I just want to confirm that we won't be cleaning roadside gutters."

Mrs. Frempong confirmed, "We will not be cleaning the gutters. We will leave those up to the professionals, not because most of the gutters contain dirty water and smelly garbage, but because it would be too dangerous for the group to do. We want everybody to be safe. Safety is foremost."

She ended the discussion by saying, "We want this to be a success. Let's help make Madina Heights the cleanest town in the Greater Accra Region or the country for that matter."

Adwoa responded, "That would be second cleanest because Dzorwulu will be the cleanest."

Mrs. Frempong said, "That's the spirit! Who else is not from Madina Heights? That way we can make it a challenge for all towns and end up having the whole of Greater Accra Region clean. That would be wonderful, wouldn't it?"

Before the cleanup event, the group had a discussion about waste. They thought of ways to reduce, recycle and repurpose waste. Adwoa was very interested in this topic, especially in reducing waste and in particular, plastic waste.

She pointed out, "Even when plastic waste reaches the landfill, it still remains a problem because it does not degrade easily. In addition to the huge amount of plastic garbage, we have limited landfill space. If improvements are to continue in keeping our environment clean, then there will be a greater need for landfill space."

Another MHES member suggested, "People are aware of the advantages of plastic and that is why it is so widely used. So until there is an **environmentally friendly** and cheap alternative available, people will not cease to use as much plastic. Already we are seeing the use of bio-degradable plastic."

Another member added, "If we must use plastic, then we should focus on recycling and repurposing it to avoid having it end up in landfill sites and in water bodies."

The debate continued for some time. Mrs. Frempong said, "The other group that I am part of is focusing on the repurposing end of the cycle. We are in discussions with a company that reprocesses used plastic into small pellets that are then used to manufacture other products."

She went on to say, "We don't necessarily have to choose one strategy to eliminate plastic from landfills. We can try to reduce it at every stage of its life cycle. We can look at ways to reduce the amount of plastic used in the first place by opting for alternative products. We can reuse things like bags and allow goods to be reused by someone else when we no longer have use for them. We can also recycle plastic by reprocessing or converting it into something new or similar.

"Better yet, as mentioned earlier, biodegradable plastic is available and should be used whenever possible. Sooner or later, with ongoing research they will come up with a substitute product. If we attack the problem in these different ways, we could drastically reduce the amount of plastic that ends up in landfills and hopefully eliminate the problem some day."

Kofi looked at Adwoa who he noticed was often asking questions and offering great comments. He didn't want Adwoa to steal the show. After all, he was the president.

He asked, "Would households be responsible for separating the garbage before making it available for pick up? If so, our current waste management system is not set up like that."

Mrs. Frempong replied, "That's correct. Our town's waste management system is not set up that way, but there are places where co-mingled garbage is picked up and then separated at the garbage depot. It wasn't so long ago that recycle programmes were implemented as part of waste management systems. We can work with the system that we have unless the companies responsible for waste change their policy.

"For example, you can have a private company handle recyclable garbage only and pick it up directly from households and businesses. Don't forget that plans can be devised to suit our circumstances as long as they are efficient and effective."

Kofi added, "The difference is that in the pre-sorted garbage system, more than one bin would be required and people would have to be made aware of exactly what goes into which garbage bin. But once the system is put in place and people are informed beforehand, they will quickly get used to it. This gets the public more involved in the process and their participation will heighten their awareness and contribution to keeping the environment clean. The other way would put the full responsibility on the waste management company."

Adwoa reminded them, "It wouldn't be too difficult. It would be like what we went through at school. Before we didn't use recycle bins and now we are all used to them. Now it's normal; it has become a habit."

Mrs. Frempong said, "These are some of the issues and solutions regarding waste management. We will have to wait for changes from the town, region or private enterprises. In the meantime, our schools will follow the programme that we have implemented and hopefully we can expand it to other public schools in Madina Heights. Private schools would be welcome to adopt similar programmes."

After the meeting was adjourned, Kofi approached Adwoa in the hallway and said, "You know Adwoa, you should rather be focusing your thoughts on fundraising. Fundraising around here is nearly impossible. Maybe you are used to the easy Canadian way, but that is not how we do things here. Our people spend money differently and many do not have extra to spare. Good luck!" he mocked.

"Don't worry. Fundraising won't be a problem for me. I am concerned about our environment as well," Adwoa retorted.

"We'll see!" Kofi said, *green* with envy.

Leading up to the cleanup day, the group's cleanup activities were broadcast by local radio stations and members sought help from family, friends and volunteers.

MHES received donations of gloves, disposable surgical masks, aprons, rakes, garbage bags and drinking water from businesses. They ordered T-shirts with the MHES inscription on them to wear on cleanup day.

The fundraising team that Adwoa led, planned to raise funds through the sale of secondhand clothes and a bake sale. They also sold specially made bumper stickers that read *"Keep MH Clean."* As part of the fundraising activities, the schools collected recycled plastic bottles, bags and containers and sold the waste to a recycling company. The money from the sale of the recycled waste was used to help purchase garbage bins.

The fundraising activities took place under a tent in the yard of one of the schools. On that day, throughout the event there was a steady stream of people coming to buy stuff. The baked goods sold out first since much of it was pre-ordered. Lots of bumper stickers were sold and additional quantities were arranged to be sold ongoing at a couple of gas stations. The only problem was that the used clothing wasn't selling as well as expected.

Towards the end of the event, a gentleman was scouring over the secondhand clothes. He picked out some items of various sizes and for different sexes. Adwoa sensed that he wanted to select more items but something was holding him back; he seemed unsure but didn't want to pass up the opportunity.

Adwoa asked him, "Please sir, may I help you?"

The gentleman confessed, "Nice! Want some for wife to sell in market."

Adwoa, realizing that he was struggling to speak English, similar to her struggles with Twi, was patient. She asked, "Is she in the market now?"

The man replied, "Yes, can't come now."

Adwoa suggested, "Call her... Show picture... Video on your phone..."

The man said, "Yes, yes! Good! I show her." He called his wife on the phone and started to video record the used clothing.

The man's wife was very interested in the clothes and asked about prices. Adwoa decided to persist, remembering her visit to the Makola Market with her Ma. She figured that it would be better to get rid of the clothing rather than to hang on to them and maybe end up having to give them away. Today she was going to be the "chief bargainer."

She called over Mr. Boateng to help with the transaction. The man indicated that he was interested in buying all the clothes if the price was right.

Mr. Boateng called out, "Kofi, please come and give us a hand here."

He instructed Kofi to help determine the cost by the individual pieces of clothing. After the price was calculated, the man exclaimed, "No, no, too much. Half!"

Adwoa was ready for a deal and neither Mr. Boateng nor Kofi could speak the man's dialect either, so she wasted no time and blurted out, "Daddy, just for you, big discount! ...Real cheap since Madam will sell. Forty percent off... Almost half price!"

The man accepted the offer readily.

Afterwards Mr. Boateng said, "We did very well! We literally cleaned up today. Pardon the pun."

Adwoa replied, "We can't argue with that. Right Kofi?"

Kofi ignored her.

14

Keeping
It Clean

On the cleanup day, MHES group members came wearing their MHES T-shirts and caps. They were equipped with the appropriate cleaning gear. Members were put into small groups which were assigned team leaders. The groups were then spread out in various areas to clean up specific places in the community.

Many volunteers joined the members to clean up—some of them doing it spontaneously. Members feverishly combed the grounds for garbage. Each small group had garbage bags to fill. The bags were collected by trucks that were provided by some businesses for the event. They collected plastic garbage separately.

The cleanup group took a well-deserved lunch break after working continuously in the sun.

They were provided with water and snacks, again courtesy of local organizations and volunteers.

What was most encouraging was that people throughout the community took the opportunity to clean their own premises and surroundings, making it a unified effort. They realized that even if their homes were clean and public places weren't, they would be exposed to the same health hazards as others in the community.

During the cleanup, Adwoa was surprised at the extent of plastic waste. Apart from plastic being used for its liquid-resistant properties, she found that many small boutiques and shops used custom branded plastic bags for their merchandise. Adwoa noticed the large amount of plastic containers like jerry cans which were used for storing things like water and gas. Plastic utensils, especially basins were widely used and traders used them to stock sale items to carry on their heads. She felt that plastic waste was an issue of high priority that required an urgent solution.

Members ended up working all day to complete the cleanup. MHES gained great exposure during the cleanup event and received praise for their work. After the event, eight more students became members.

Following the major community cleanup, garbage bins were placed in strategic locations throughout the community. They were placed in markets, bus and tro tro stations, at schools and at roadsides in high traffic areas. Some vehicles used for public transportation were provided with wastepaper bins. Regular garbage pick-up was scheduled for once a week in Madina Heights.

MHES encouraged its members and the whole community to cooperate and use the bins to store garbage and refrain from throwing garbage around, especially in gutters where it clogged drains. They also asked all public and religious organizations and some private organizations to join them in their efforts by promoting and practicing good sanitation.

Each month on National Sanitation Day, group members were to be actively involved in cleanup efforts at home and at school. Competition between various areas in the community helped in getting more people to participate in the programme and in developing a greater sense of pride in the community.

15

A True Legend

A few days later, Adwoa asked Esi, "Did you remove a cup containing fruit from my room?"

Esi replied, "No. I didn't remove a plastic cup from your room."

Adwoa then asked her mother, "Ma, did you by any chance remove a cup with fruit from my room?"

Faith said, "No, I didn't. Look carefully. It must be there."

When Adwoa checked with her dad, he too said that he had not removed the cup from her room. It was puzzling. It was a mystery how the cup containing the fruit disappeared; a mystery that Adwoa intended to solve. She had to get to the bottom of the whereabouts of the cup of ghost fruit.

Faith helped her to look for the cup. They looked all over Adwoa's room but couldn't find the cup. Faith began to tidy the bookcase which they both had already searched for the cup. The papers that had rested against the cup were lying flat on the bookshelf. When Faith removed the papers, the bottom pages were sitting in a blob of something. Adwoa noticed that the blob and her papers were stained the same colour as the rotting ghost fruit. She became suspicious, confused and frightened.

Faith asked, "What's this stuff? It's ruining your papers."

As Faith was about to remove the soiled papers and help clean up the mess, Adwoa shouted, "No, Ma please don't touch it!"

Adwoa told her, "The ghost fruit were turning into this purple colour, so the blob may have something to do with them."

"Where is the rest of the fruit and who took them out of the plastic cup?" Faith asked.

The cup was nowhere in sight. Sam came home shortly afterwards and they told him about the missing cup of fruit and the blob.

Sam asked Adwoa, "Are you absolutely sure that nobody removed the cup of fruit from your room?"

Adwoa replied, "Ma, Esi and you all say that you did not remove it and neither did I."

"We've got a backward thief around here?" Sam joked.

"A backward thief, Dad?" asked Adwoa, trying not to smile too much during what she thought was a rather serious dilemma.

"Yes, a thief who leaves porcelain mugs and crystal glasses in our cupboards and rather takes a plastic cup! How confused!" Sam tried to make light of the situation in his usual way. Then he straightened his face. "Really, there has got to be an explanation." He put on a pair of gloves, then placed the sticky papers in a container and proceeded to clean the stain from the bookshelf.

Adwoa asked, "Dad, what are you going to do with the soiled papers?"

Sam answered, "Put them on the wall as art."

"Dad!" Adwoa sighed.

119

"No, I'll take them to the lab tomorrow and have them tested. Maybe the substance doesn't have anything to do with the cup of fruit."

Adwoa was consumed with thoughts of what happened to the missing cup. At night, she became restless and couldn't sleep. She tossed and turned thinking about ghosts and evil curses that she must have brought upon herself and her family. She wasn't so sure of things anymore; neither was she feeling lucky. Her previous sound reasoning gave way to fear.

Adwoa began to see every misfortune that she encountered since the fruit went missing, as part of a terrible curse. Maybe the curse was the cause of her losing her purse and maybe it was why she was not feeling so well lately. Maybe that's why Kofi didn't like her. Worse was the increased frequency of power outages which left her at the mercy of the evil ones in the darkness of her room at night. *Maybe I should talk to the pastor and ask for prayers to protect me from the curses that are about to happen*, Adwoa thought.

If only I could get the curse reversed, Adwoa wished, thinking that her parents would have to get help from a fetish priest. She even secretly poured libation in an effort to appease the gods and ask for forgiveness from her ancestors.

What if things got so bad that everyone started to avoid me? By then, the community would surely expel me to a witch camp, Adwoa feared. Despite her parents' assurances that she was not under a curse, she was filled with fright.

Each passing day Adwoa waited to find out if her father got the test results for the substance in the blob. It seemed to take forever to get back the results. About a month later when he received the results from the lab, Sam called from work to tell them about the results. He was so excited that he couldn't wait until he got home to give them the news.

Sam told them excitedly, "I have incredible news. We got back the test results today. Now we know why it is called the ghost fruit. It is because the fruit can make itself and things like plastic disappear into thin air. The results from the lab confirmed that the ghost fruit virtually ate the cup."

Adwoa asked, "You mean that ghost fruit destroy plastic?"

"Yes, they do," Sam confirmed.

Adwoa said hysterically, "That's the solution to our plastic problem!"

"This is really a big discovery. It's unbelievable!" Faith remarked.

Adwoa said, "That means that plastic sachets, bags, bottles and containers will no longer have to be disposed of in landfills. Plastic that is already in landfills can now be made to decompose."

"Not so fast! Lots more research and testing will have to be done to confirm the initial findings. They have to look at any possible side effects of using ghost fruit. Even then, there must be enough quantities of ghost fruit produced before they can be used commercially. All of that will take time," Sam cautioned. "But it is a great discovery none-the-less."

"A scientist from the lab will go to the villages around Samandua Forest to interview some native traditional medicine men. She learned that they secretly use the ghost fruit in herbal medicines. The medicine men believe that ghost fruit have healing powers but they don't know exactly what kind of powers and how potent they are."

"So there is some kind of truth to the legend after all. If knowledge about the beneficial use of the fruit hadn't been kept a secret, this discovery could have been made long ago," Adwoa regretted.

Adwoa couldn't wait to tell her friends, especially Nii Isaac, about the findings of the ghost fruit. She wondered what other natural treasures were hidden in plain sight, just waiting to be discovered. Adwoa was relieved to know that she wasn't under a curse after all. She felt that everything and everyone on Earth had a special purpose just like the old lady at the airport had said.

Adwoa wasted no time in telling Mrs. Frempong about the test results and discovery, "Mrs. Frempong, I know that you would want to hear this. Remember when we went on the field trip to Samandua Forest? Well, I brought home some ghost fruit in a plastic cup and it all turned into a blob. My dad got the blob tested at a lab…"

Mrs. Frempong couldn't take the suspense any longer, as Adwoa was bubbling with excitement. She interrupted, "and…"

Adwoa blurted out, "…And the ghost fruit ate the plastic cup."

"Ate the plastic?" Mrs. Frempong repeated.

"Yes, ghost fruit destroy plastic. I left them in a plastic cup and they dissolved the cup."

"Oh, that is excellent news! You must tell me more about it. Keep me informed!" Mrs. Frempong said with enthusiasm.

Fundraising
With a Twist

So far, MHES had participated in a country activity by planting trees in Samandua Forest and its members had also performed community cleanup. At the school level they had improved waste management by not littering and separating recyclable garbage from regular garbage. The individual schools had addressed efficiency in terms of not wasting school supplies, water and electricity. Now the schools were to come up with their individual projects for greening their schools.

Madina Heights JHS made plans to construct badly needed outdoor recreational facilities to ease congestion in the school building during recess and to provide students with comfortable outdoor seating and other amenities that were environmentally friendly.

The three public schools were experiencing problems with water supply and it was affecting their WASH (Water, Sanitation and Hygiene) programmes to varying degrees. The water situation was urgent and posed a threat to students' health and wellbeing. MHES decided to address the problem of the erratic water supply by developing rain harvesting systems at the schools.

Before the project got underway, MHES wanted to secure funding through fundraising before the end-of-term exams and before students went on vacation.

Adwoa thought long and hard about achieving the group's short-term and long-term fundraising goals. Mrs. Frempong wanted to avoid having to raise funds for every event when it occurred. Since it was the group's first year, she felt that it should have some funds set aside.

Adwoa thought of the various ways they used to raise funds in Canada. She thought about doing a car wash event but figured that it wouldn't be as productive because a lot of people had their vehicles washed at home. Although most gas stations didn't have car washing bays, the availability and cost of water to wash the cars would not make it worthwhile.

Adwoa and her team got ready for the large-scale fundraiser, having been encouraged by the success of the first one. They were expecting great results. They scheduled two main fundraising events: a raffle and a fair. They also planned to ask for donations directly from the public. Fundraising was to be completed by the end of the second term.

The fundraising team was hoping that the prizes for the raffle would generate a lot of interest. Mrs. Frempong would secure donations of valuable electronic prizes for the raffle from businesses. The first prize was a handheld computer. The second prize was a cell phone. The third prize was a wireless Bluetooth earpiece.

Selling tickets to families proved to be more challenging than Adwoa expected. For starters, unlike in Toronto where you could easily walk up to a house or enter an apartment building, ring the doorbell and speak to the resident, in Ghana it took more effort. Since most houses in Madina Heights were gated or located within gated communities, gaining access to people was much more difficult unless they were reached at shops or markets. For safety reasons and because of their ages, members had to be accompanied by adults when they were selling raffle tickets.

It had been decided that students living in gated communities or that had reasons to be there, should approach residents in those communities for support. Reaching other residents at their homes would prove just as difficult because some residences had a security guard that there was no chance of getting past. If there wasn't a security guard, then the first contact would be a houseboy or housegirl. They made getting to talk with heads of households difficult or almost impossible. Adwoa had one such encounter for the first time one Saturday afternoon.

Adwoa was accompanied by Esi who rang a doorbell from outside a gate. When the houseboy reached the gate, he opened it slightly and stared at them as if to ask: *What do you want?*

Adwoa greeted him, "Good afternoon."

The houseboy replied, "Good afternoon."

Adwoa asked, "Please, may we speak to Madam?"

The houseboy replied. "Is Madam expecting you?"

Adwoa replied, "No, but she will be happy to see us."

He asked, "Why so?"

Adwoa said, "We have something to tell her; something that will interest her."

The houseboy asked, "Who should I tell her is asking to see her?"

Adwoa replied, "Adwoa."

He said, "So when I tell Madam that Adwoa is at the gate to see her and she asks, "What for?" I should tell her that Adwoa has something interesting to tell her? And you think that Madam won't be annoyed with me for disturbing her?"

Like him, Esi had just passed her teenage years. She intervened, "Please just give Madam the message and we will wait."

The houseboy toyed with them, "Are you sure that you aren't here to beg for something."

"We are not beggars," Adwoa chided.

"Selling or begging: it's the same thing," the houseboy nagged.

By this time, Esi was running out of patience and rang the doorbell again. This infuriated the houseboy who closed the gate, locked it and turned around to go inside. Just then Adwoa and Esi could hear someone from inside the house calling him. As he hurried to go back inside the house, the front door opened and the Madam stepped outside.

She asked him, "Have you been outside all this time? I've been calling you. What is it?" The houseboy tried to explain that the girls were trying to see her. The madam shared some short words with him and motioned him inside.

Others weren't having any better luck with getting donations either. Even Mrs. Frempong was having a hard time with getting donated prizes. At this first defeat, Adwoa remembered Kofi's discouraging words. In a moment of weakness, she began to recoil into a version of her unsure self. *Maybe moving to Ghana was a big mistake. Maybe I really won't be able to raise a huge amount of funds. Maybe I came all the way here to Ghana just to embarrass myself. Maybe the ghost fruit actually did bring a curse.* "Oh! What am I going to do?" she cried.

Bulletins were posted in front each of the four schools and at the public library to advertise the fundraising events. Otherwise, advertising was by word of mouth since there wasn't a community newspaper. It was common practice for people to advertise local events by posting fliers on electricity poles but MHES chose not to create more waste. Students also advertised the events online through social media.

Most residents wanted to support the cause and help to build their community. When approached about supporting the project, people were very vocal in their opinions and were not reluctant to apportion blame for the water situation.

One man said accusingly, "This is the government's responsibility. All that our politicians do is chop our money and fill their deep pockets. That's why the children don't have enough water at school."

A trader advised, "Go to the 'honourable' Member of Parliament for Education and ask him for money. They say that education is free, yet we have to pay fees for this and fees for that and still they can't provide the schoolchildren with water to drink."

There were many such comments and expressions of frustration from people, although some of them still gave their support.

A feisty lady took the opportunity to complain about the erratic public water supply. She said, "They provide you with water when they like. Sometimes you get it four days in a week, other times it can be two days in a week. Water can come anytime—morning, noon or night. You never know when to expect it, meanwhile the price keeps going up and you still have to buy some from elsewhere."

Another trader replied after the lady spoke, "At least you have water connection. I am still waiting to get connected up till now."

Adwoa soon decided she had no choice but to try harder. She wasn't going to be defeated by a crushed spirit. One day, when she was trying to figure out the situation and what to do to turn it around, she sat in her room and thought. A voice from the past echoed in her mind. It was that of one of her former teachers in Canada, Mrs. Coxwell. Mrs. Coxwell would often tell her students: *Think outside the box. If everyone thought alike, the world would be at a standstill.*

Adwoa used to have a drawing that depicted this message on her wall to give her inspiration, but she threw it away when she was leaving for Ghana. She instantly drew a square with the word *"think"* outside of its perimeter and hung it on the wall of her room.

Adwoa also remembered what Mrs. Frempong said at one of the earlier MHES meetings about waste management. She said, "Plans can be devised to suit our circumstances as long as they are efficient and effective."

Kofi's comments too about fundraising in Ghana were proving to be true, whether or not they were well-intended. It was time for Adwoa to find new fundraising strategies for Ghana. She had to find ways to reach those people who had extra money. She thought about the fair and the large crowds that would attend; most of them would be young people.

In Canada, most high school and university students had part-time jobs and therefore had money to spend. The majority of younger students like herself would get allowance from their parents. This was not the case for most Ghanaian youth. This meant that she would have to lower her expectations for funds from the fair.

Since the fair was still in the planning stages, Adwoa thought that they could make changes whereby MHES would provide water, soft drinks and snacks, games and entertainment, everything other than cooked meals, and rather charge businesses for operating booths. Businesses that provided services would be invited to pay for booths to advertise and sell their products and services. MHES might also benefit from these business connections in the future.

Adwoa also searched the Internet for alumni of junior high and high schools in Madina Heights. She was lucky to not only find an alumnus but also to make contact with them. The former students were generous in their support of the project. Apart from raising funds from friends and family, the group advertised the events on the alumnus Facebook page. They also sent out tweets to reach supporters living outside of Madina Heights.

Adwoa had one last trick up her sleeves. Her friends and former green group in Canada had offered to assist with MHES projects. Although MHES did not decline the offer, it wanted Ghanaian youth to be in the forefront of solving their own environmental problems so it agreed to partial assistance. She decided to ask her Canadian friends and counterparts for financial assistance.

She remembered the houseboy accusing her of begging when she was asking for donations, but now she didn't mind the hardships of fundraising because it was for a great cause: protecting the environment. To her that was everything.

Now that she had a refreshed outlook and approach, Adwoa found planning for the fair to be exciting. The fair would be held before the draw of the raffle. The event was scheduled for Ghana's Independence Day anniversary on March 6th. It was a national holiday and they expected to draw a huge crowd. They planned fun activities for kids and great entertainment for adults and older people so that people could enjoy themselves. The fair would be held at one of the public schools which had a large sports field and outdoor space that was connected to a churchyard. There was plenty of space for parking and tro tros passed the fairgrounds regularly. Everything else would depend on the weather.

The activities planned for the fair included face-painting, games, rides, a bounce house and a slide. There would be lots of food, including cakes, bofrots (a sweet, round treat like donut balls), kelewele, ice cream, yogurt, chin chin and meat pies, plantain and banana chips, sugar cane, ground and tiger nuts, yam fries and all kinds of drinks. There was a clown, stilt walkers and other performers wearing beautiful costumes and nice music.

MHES met on the Sunday afternoon before the fair to go over members' assigned duties at the fair and to help get the fairgrounds ready. Members filled balloons with air and decorated tables at the front of the stage. Adwoa began to feel excited while helping with the preparations. Other people were busy unloading chairs and tables and setting up the tents. There were four large tents under which food items were to be sold. There was also one small tent that would serve as an information booth and where raffle tickets were to be sold. There was also a covered area where people were to sit in front of a stage. Garbage bins were placed around the fairgrounds.

The weather forecast predicted a sunny day.

Everything   seemed   perfect.

17

All Is Not Fair

When they were about to leave the fairgrounds the final day before the fair, Adwoa asked Kofi to grab her notepad that she had rested on one of the tables. Kofi noticed that Adwoa had some drawings on the pages.

Kofi asked, "What are these drawings for?"

Adwoa answered, "I was thinking about the discussions at our last meeting and I was trying to come up with a catchy way to promote keeping the city clean. An idea came to my mind so I drew those sketches."

Kofi scoffed, "Another Aburo Kyire idea?"

Adwoa retaliated, "Actually it's a made-in-Ghana idea."

Kofi asked, "So what is it?"

Adwoa said, "Never mind!"

Kofi, Adwoa and Charity continued to walk home together. The topic drifted to the schools that had members in MHES and the state of some of the schools.

Kofi said, "You students from the private school wouldn't understand what some students at the public schools have to do to survive. Do you know that some can't afford lunch or their school fees, much less tickets to the fair? They are not rich like you."

Charity responded, "Hey Kofi, Kofi! What is it with you today? What is your problem?"

Kofi replied, "I am just saying that there are poor people both in MHES and at school who cannot afford things."

Charity said, "That may be so but why are you trying to blame us for that? There are poor people everywhere."

Adwoa weighed into the conversation after letting it sink in, "But I am not rich." After hesitating she added, "Neither am I poor." I am somewhere in between and I have nothing to do with that. I feel bad about those students' situations, but what do you expect me to do?"

Kofi answered, "Nothing, just forget about it."

Charity concluded, "How can we forget about it? Why are you trying to blame us for the students' poverty because we go to private school? That's not fair."

Adwoa quarreled, "Kofi, you should check what you are saying! You know that my brother goes to public secondary school so if you look at it from that side, then I am also poor. We are trying to raise funds so do you expect us to give away tickets? The price of children's tickets is already reduced. Everybody won't and can't come to the fair."

They continued walking to their homes. Adwoa was disturbed by what Kofi said and continued to think about it at home. Faith noticed that Adwoa was unusually quiet.

Faith inquired, "What's wrong?"

Adwoa said, "Nothing."

Faith said, "Are you sure you don't want to talk about it? You look as if something is troubling you."

Adwoa reluctantly told her about the conversation that she, Kofi and Charity had.

Faith asked, "Did something happen before the conversation to bring it on?"

Adwoa said, "We were working in different areas after our group met so I asked Kofi to bring along my notepad from his area where I left it. I didn't like the way he referred to my drawings as an 'Aburo Kyire idea.'"

Faith said, "Sometimes people say 'Aburo Kyire' but they don't mean it as something negative."

Adwoa said, "I know. They often refer to me as 'Aburo Kyire' at school so I am used to it, but it is the way he said it."

Faith asked, "Are you sure that you are not offended when they refer to you as a foreigner? What did you mean by 'made-in-Ghana idea?'"

Adwoa explained, "I remember well when I first arrived in Ghana that I saw banners, billboards and other signs advertising products like phone services along the roadside. I thought that it would be a good idea to make similar

142

advertisements to remind people to keep the city clean so I made some sketches on my notepad."

Faith responded, "Hmm, maybe something else was bothering Kofi or maybe he was just having a bad day."

Adwoa said, "What bothers me more is when he refers to me as rich. I know that there are poor people around, maybe too many, but every country has poor people. It is like when we were in Toronto and whenever they showed African children on television, it was usually poor children in rags and now that I am here rather, I am being accused of being rich."

Faith replied, "Yes there is a lot of poverty in Ghana, but some of the poor people are richer in spirit than some rich people anywhere. Poverty is a big problem. You shouldn't worry yourself about what anybody says or thinks.

"Now, cheer up and forget about what happened today. You can't go to the fair tomorrow looking gloomy and sad, especially when you have to sell raffle tickets and tell people about your group. Maybe some time later when things quiet down, you can discuss the incident with Kofi."

143

At the fair, Adwoa spent two hours at the information booth where she helped to sell raffle tickets, gave out information about the project and MHES, and answered queries. She was delighted to see her fellow students there. Once the music started, crowds began to fill the place quickly. Midway during the fair, the grounds were packed with people.

When Adwoa was free from her duties at the information booth, she joined some of her friends and visited a number of booths and activities. She saw the younger kids having fun in the bounce house. Adwoa passed the beautifully costumed stilt walkers as she headed to the stage area where the teenagers were listening to a school band perform and it later turned into a karaoke.

Many adults volunteered by helping with the activities. Others were taking care of their kids and enjoying the atmosphere. Since her return to Ghana, Adwoa had attended a few festivals but she liked the fair better because it was an event mostly for children. It reminded her a little of going to the Exhibition Place back in Toronto.

Adwoa was happy.

The fundraising activities raised above the targeted amount.

Forever Green

The remainder of the empty space in Samandua Forest was replanted with forbidden trees. The reforestation programme expanded to other areas and acres of forbidden trees were planted.

MHES continued to encourage people to dispose of their garbage properly and to reduce the use of plastic goods. The group continued to vigorously promote the use of personal drinking water bottles since they were reusable, created less waste and were less costly.

Groups similar to MHES were formed in various communities to work to protect the environment and to build their communities. Some MHES members went away to senior high schools outside of Madina Heights but a few members moved on to high schools in the town and opted to remain members.

Madina Heights was regarded as the leading green community in Ghana. MHES continued to work towards its vision of improved environmental standards resulting in good sanitation, a continuous supply of electricity and clean water, and the protection of Ghana's natural resources. MHES kept its focus on spreading awareness to the youth and preparing them for responsible environmental stewardship for a progressive Ghana.

By the time Adwoa's grandmother came to spend time with her family at the end of the school year, Adwoa had decided what to do about the gold nugget. She confided to her what she had decided to do and asked her Grandma to take her to the jeweller that had given the highest appraisal value. Her Grandma arranged for the driver to take them to the jeweller to sell the nugget of gold.

Afterwards, they were driven to the office of Trees for Life where Adwoa donated all of the money from the sale of the nugget towards buying seedlings of forbidden trees for the reforestation programme.

Everyone was proud of Adwoa for the choice that she made. Her father was especially proud of her. Sam said to Adwoa, "I knew that I could count on you to do the right thing. I am very proud of you."

One day, as Adwoa sat there in one of MHES's meetings, she realized she was learning so much about what it meant to be "green." It wasn't just the formula she had come to know in Canada. It was that each part of the world had some green issues that were different. Even similar issues were addressed differently. The most pressing environmental issues in Ghana and Africa were somewhat different from those in Canada and North America.

In Ghana, the main environmental issues related to poor sanitation, access to clean water for the majority of people, waste that was changing the landscape and creating health and safety hazards. It was polluted water destroying helpless communities, galamsey and its destruction of natural resources and much, much more. In Canada the main environmental issues were air, water and hazardous waste pollution, climate change, conservation of species and energy.

Countries were striving to be green but in different ways and at different paces, resulting in *shades of green.* There were many green opportunities in Ghana in helping to protect the environment. This meant that with certainty, there was a place and a purpose for Adwoa in Ghana.

On the Sunday just before the start of their long vacation, Ebo and Adwoa were relaxing in the verandah at home and chatting with their friends on their phones.

Sam called out from inside the house before he reached the front door, "Has anyone seen African Canadians around here?"

Ebo and Adwoa looked at each other and rolled their eyes playfully. When Sam reached the verandah, followed by Faith, he exclaimed, "Oh here you are! You are here together but separate, each one on his phone."

He turned, looked at Faith and said, "You still think that now is a good time to tell them?"

Faith replied looking worried, "I guess now is as good a time as any."

By now, Ebo and Adwoa were afraid of what would come next. Maybe their parents were going to have a baby or someone close had died. They looked at their parents intently.

Sam cleared his throat and said, "Guys, your mother and I have an announcement. We could be moving from Ghana in about six months."

There was a resounding and expressive, "But Dad!" as both Adwoa and Ebo objected and stormed off.

Before entering the house, Adwoa turned and asked wishfully, "Back to Canada?"

Sam replied, "No, to Germany!"

Adwoa slammed the door and Sam yelled, "Gotcha! …Just joking!"

Sam was proud that he not only got them good but that he and Faith got to sit in the chairs in the verandah.

Faith snickered. Adwoa and Ebo laughed too. Though Adwoa was relieved, she suddenly realized it didn't matter where in the world she went because with family, faith and purpose, no matter where she was, she had it all.

The End

Glossary

acclimatize to adjust or adapt to a new climate, place or situation

biodegradable capable of being broken down by living things rather than remaining as waste in the same form (or a harmful form)

desertification the transformation of land, once suitable for agriculture, into desert. It can result from climate change or from human practices such as deforestation and overgrazing

environmentally-friendly a term that refers to goods and services, laws, guidelines and policies that promise reduced, minimal, or no harm to ecosystems or the environment

green a term that refers to protecting the environment or limiting damage to it. The term describes issues that affect the environment, places that are protected in the environment and people who care about the environment.

fossil fuel a source of energy that is formed from the accumulated remains of living organisms (plants and animals) that were buried in the earth millions of years ago. Pressure, heat and time allow the organic matter to transform into one of the three major types of fossil fuels, which are coal, oil and natural gas

galamsey a term used to refer to illegal mining of precious metals and stones

hydroelectricity energy in the form of electricity, produced by movement of water. It is usually made with dams that block a river to make a reservoir or collect water that is pumped there. When the water is released, the pressure behind the dam forces the water down pipes that lead to a turbine. Hydroelectricity relies on water, which is a clean, renewable energy source

potable water water that is safe to drink or to use for food preparation, without risk of health problems

renewable energy energy that is collected from renewable resources, which are naturally replenished on a human timescale, such as sunlight, wind, rain, tides, waves, and geothermal heat

trade winds air that blows from the northeast to the southwest, back toward the equator. These are the prevailing easterly winds that circle the earth near the equator

About the Author

It was while on a work assignment in western Canada as an accountant that Judith did some soul searching about her true calling in life. She had a passion to help impoverished children, but wasn't sure of the best means of accomplishing this. Her other growing interest in environmental issues was heightened through her travels where she saw first-hand the harmful effects of environmental degradation on the poor, particularly children. Her interests in environmental issues, which are universal to all children, seem to naturally complement her desire to help children. In her quest to fulfill her calling, Judith is committed to writing environmental literature for children.

Judith believes that teaching children about the environment at an early age provides them with a solid foundation for environmental stewardship. She enlivens environmental issues by engulfing them in captivating narratives that seize the imagination and draw readers in.

Judith lives in the Greater Toronto Area in Ontario, Canada with her family.

A portion of the proceeds of book sales will support programmes for children in need.

www.ingramcontent.com/pod-product-compliance
Lightning Source LLC
Chambersburg PA
CBHW060119260626
47160CB00005B/1942